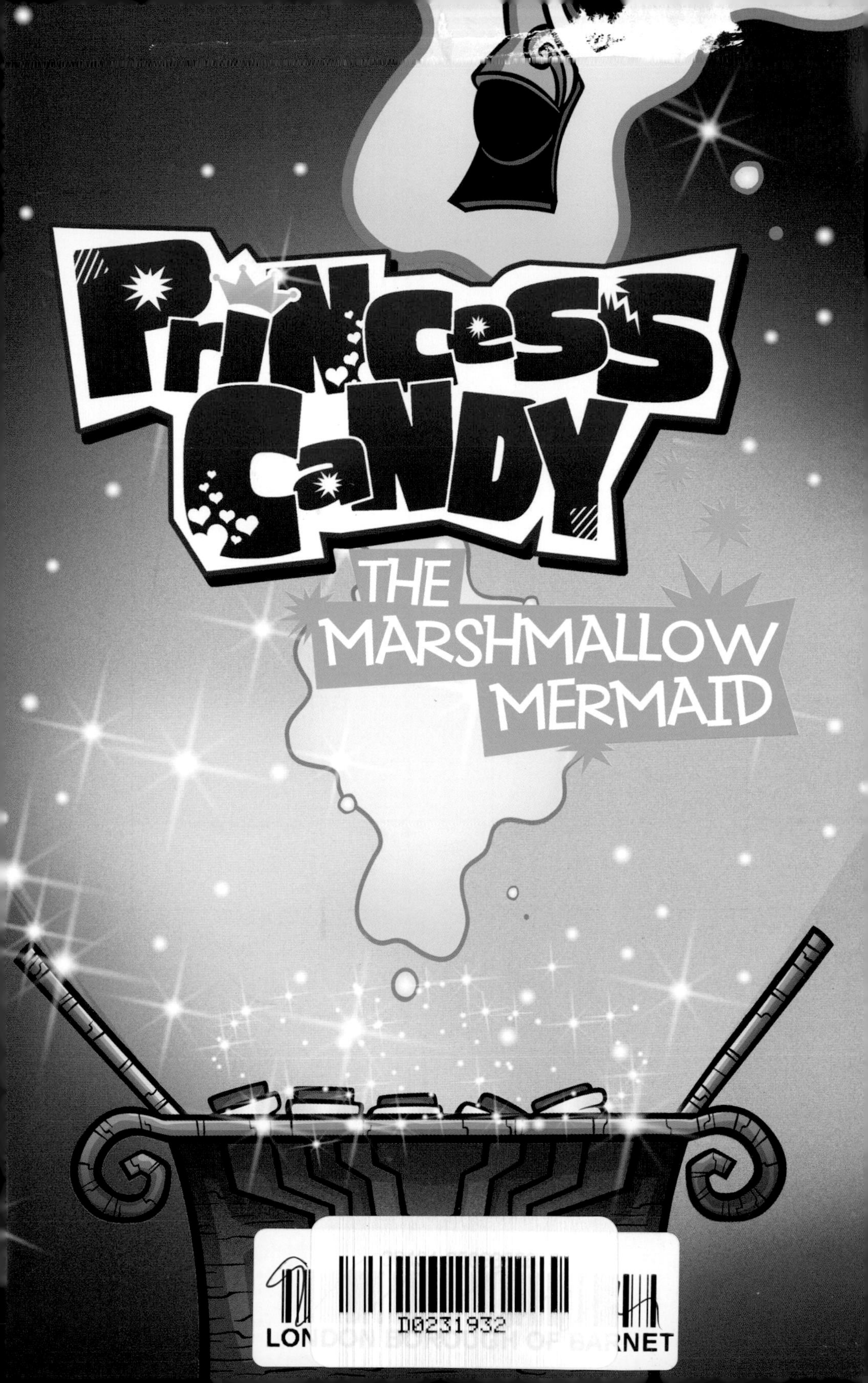
PRINCESS CANDY
THE MARSHMALLOW MERMAID

DESIGNER: **BRANN GARVEY**

SERIES EDITOR: **DONALD LEMKE**

ASSOC. EDITOR: **SEAN TULIEN**

ART DIRECTOR: **BOB LENTZ**

CREATIVE DIRECTOR: **HEATHER KINDSETH**

PRODUCTION SPECIALIST: **MICHELLE BIEDSCHEID**

Raintree is an imprint of Capstone Global Library Limited, a company incorporated in England and Wales having its registered office at 264 Banbury Road, Oxford, OX2 7DY – Registered company number: 6695582

www.raintree.co.uk
myorders@raintree.co.uk

Text © Capstone Global Library Limited 2019
The moral rights of the proprietor have been asserted

ISBN 978 1 4747 8231 9
22 21 20 19
10 9 8 7 6 5 4 3 2 1

Printed and bound in India

British Library Cataloguing in Publication Data
A full catalogue record for this book is available from the British Library.

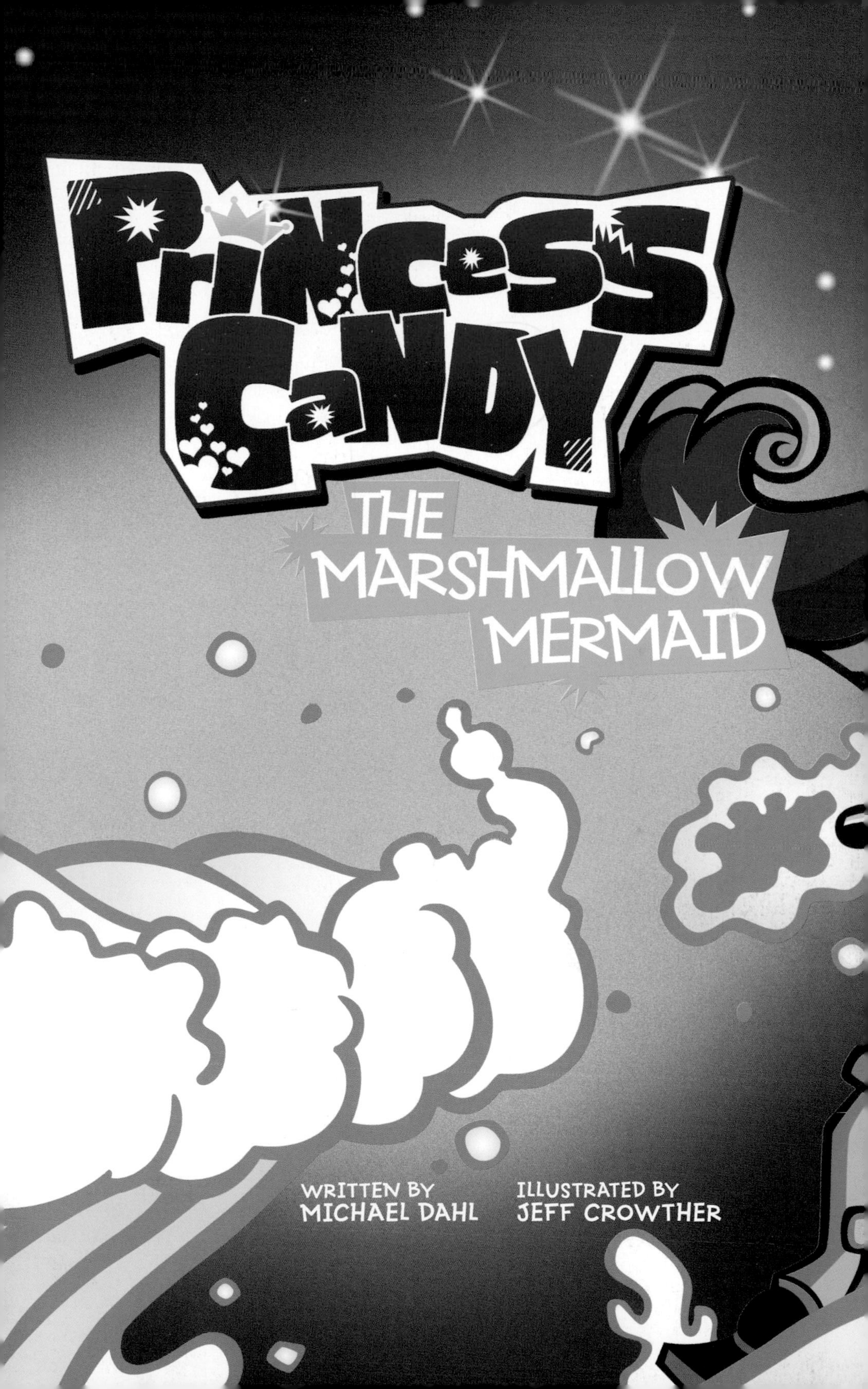
PRINCESS CANDY
THE MARSHMALLOW MERMAID
WRITTEN BY
MICHAEL DAHL
ILLUSTRATED BY
JEFF CROWTHER

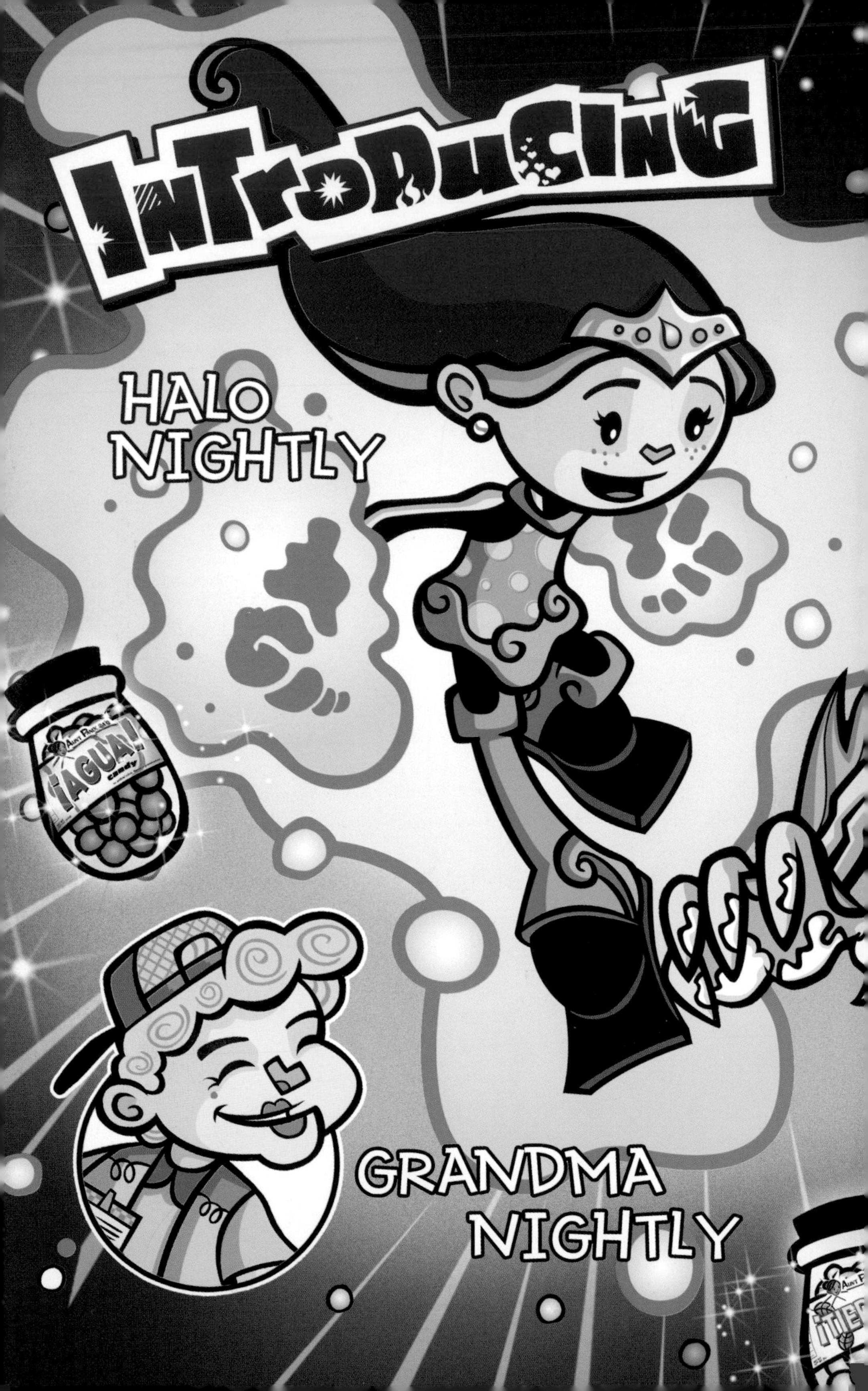
INTRODUCING
HALO NIGHTLY
GRANDMA NIGHTLY

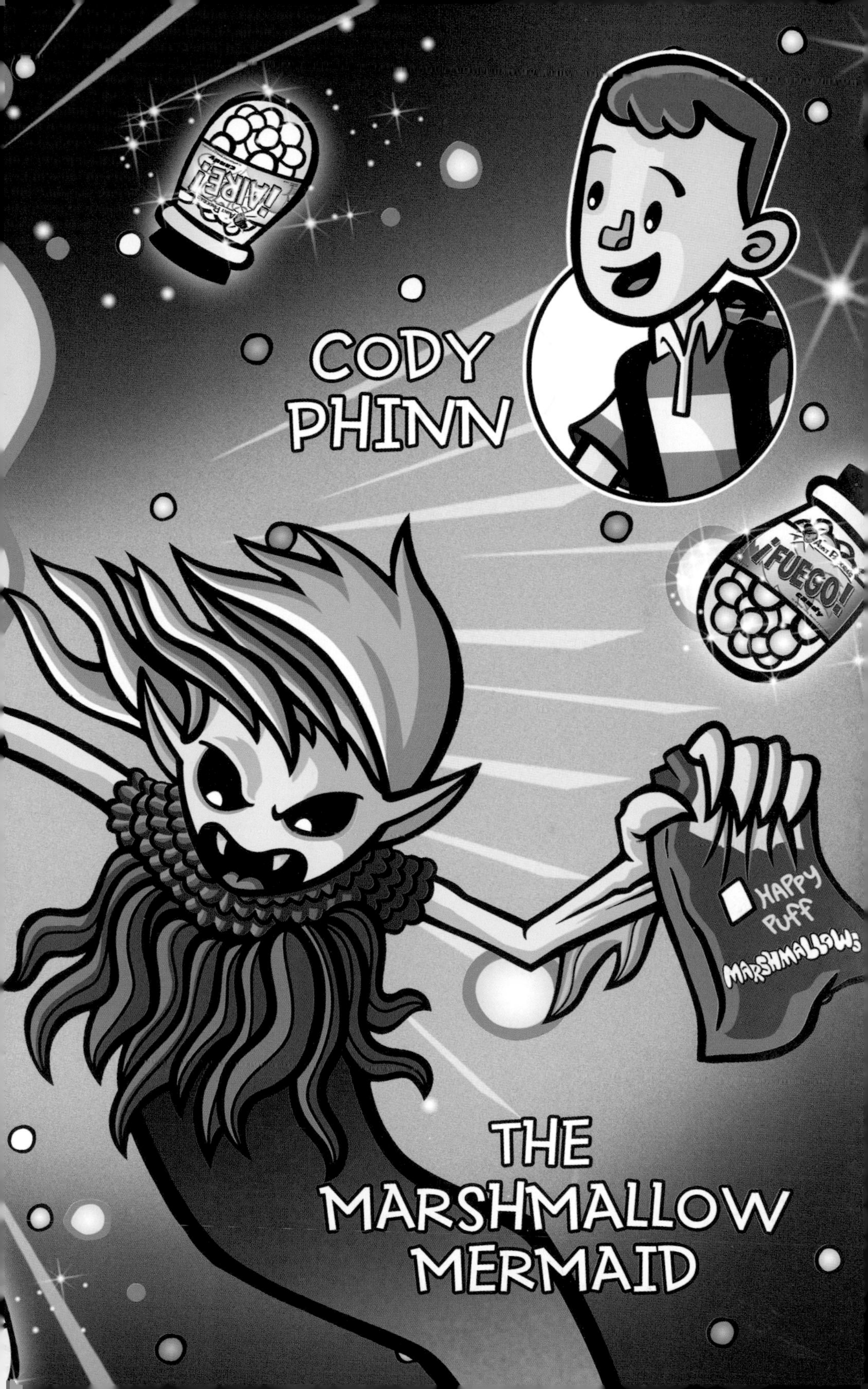

¡AIRE!
CODY PHINN
¡FUEGO!
HAPPY PUFF
MARSHMALLOWS
THE MARSHMALLOW MERMAID

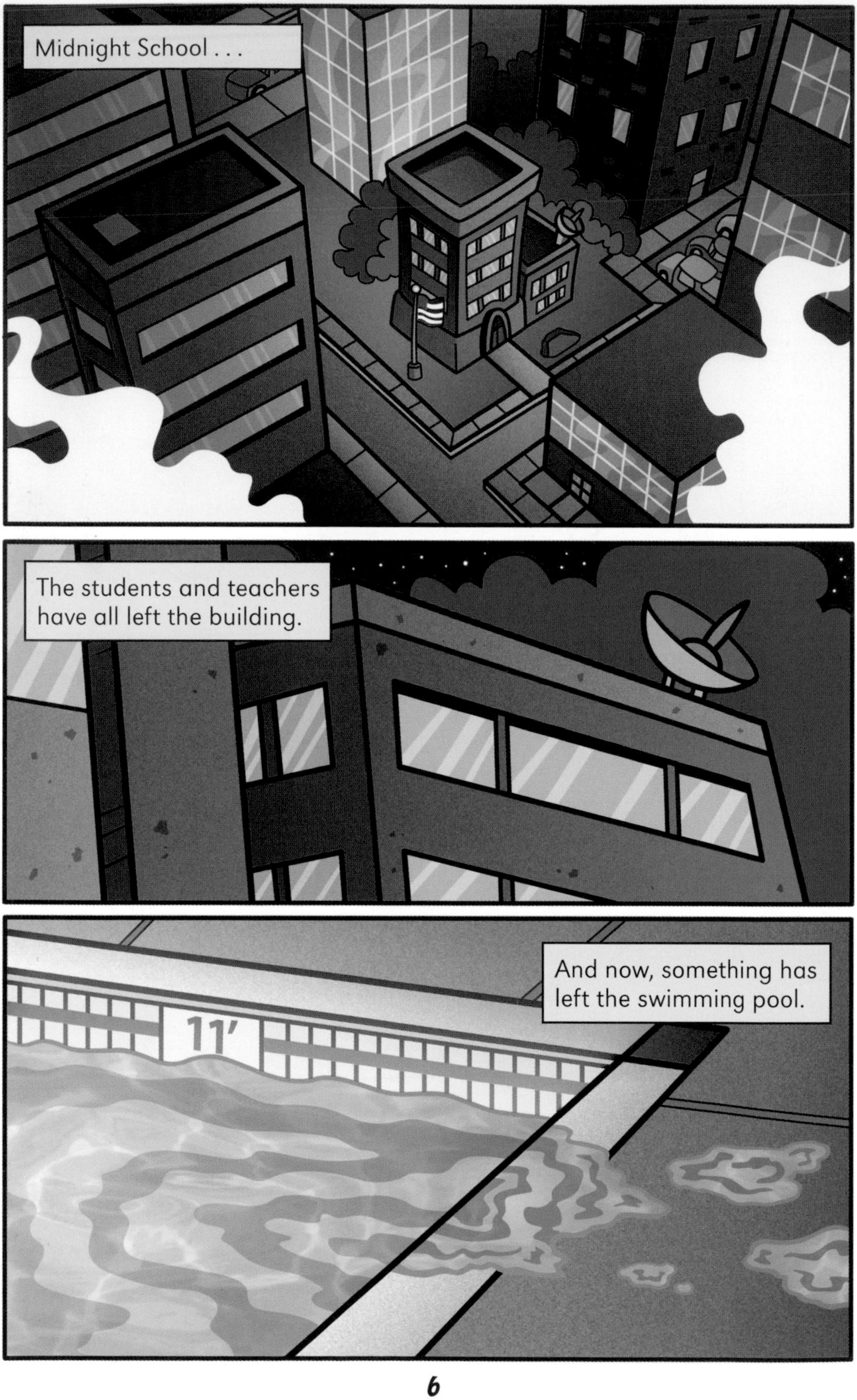
Midnight School . . .
The students and teachers have all left the building.
11'
And now, something has left the swimming pool.

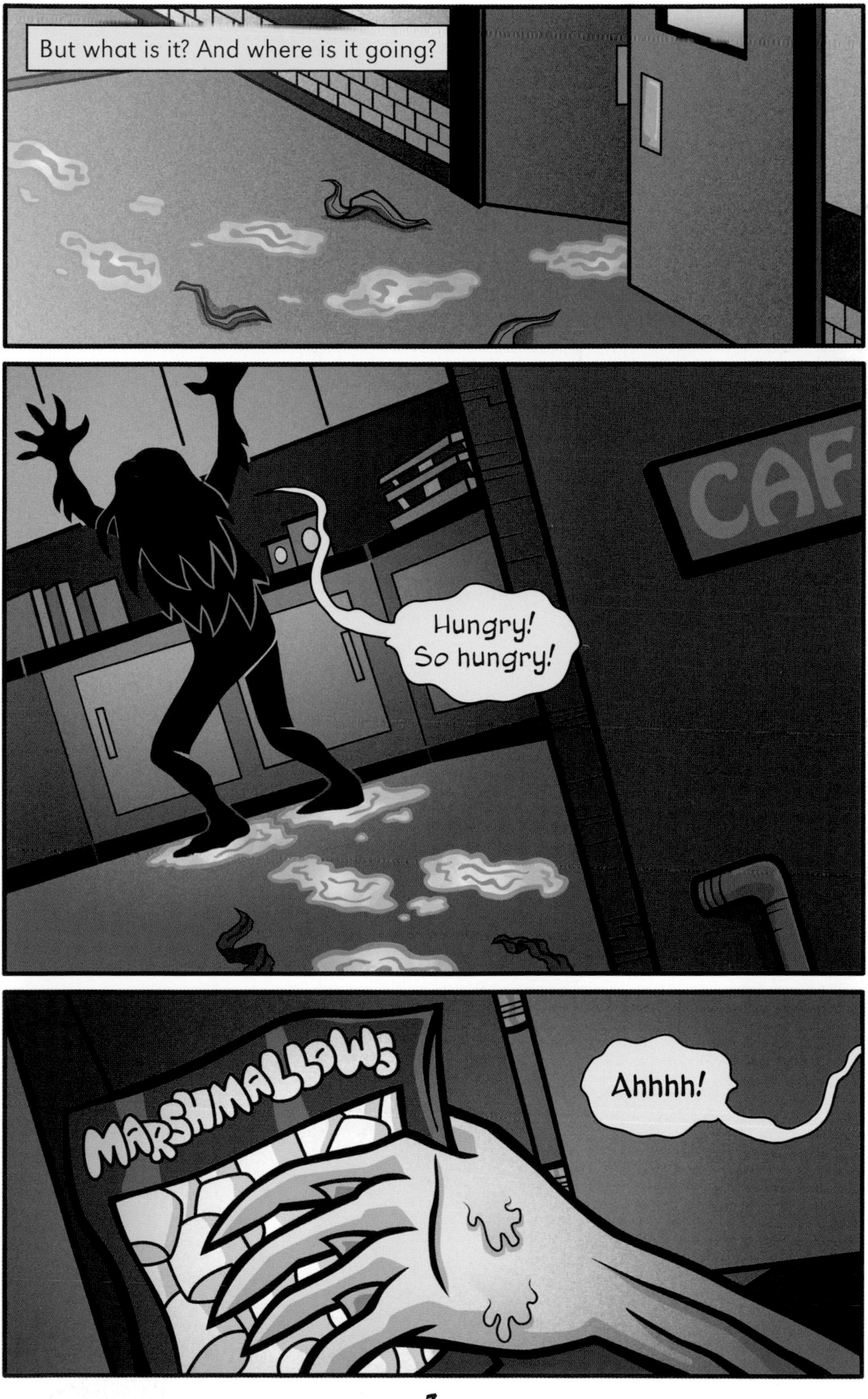
But what is it? And where is it going?
Hungry! So hungry!
CAF
MARSHMALLOWS
Ahhhh!

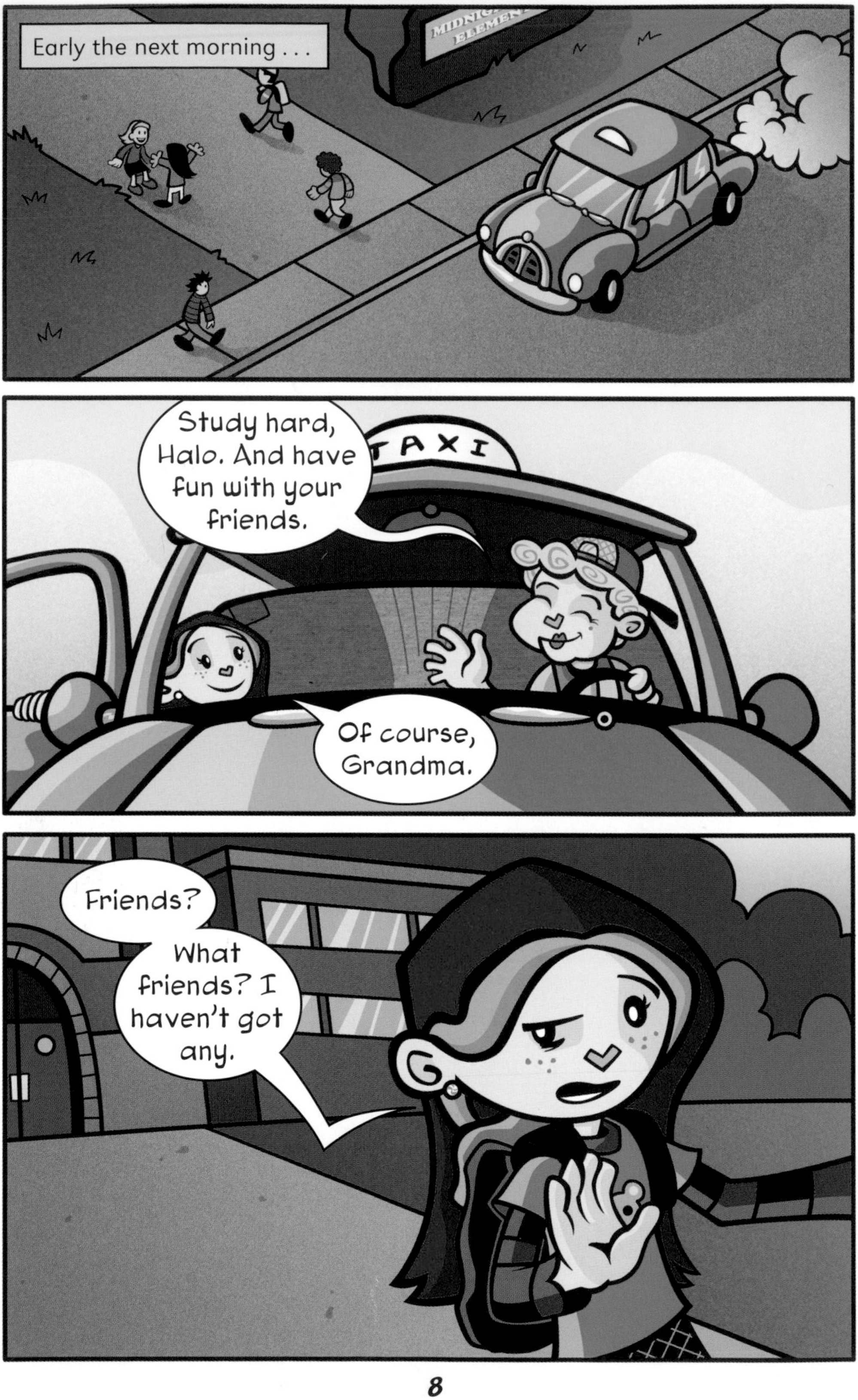
Early the next morning . . .
Study hard, Halo. And have fun with your friends.
TAXI
Of course, Grandma.
Friends?
What friends? I haven't got any.

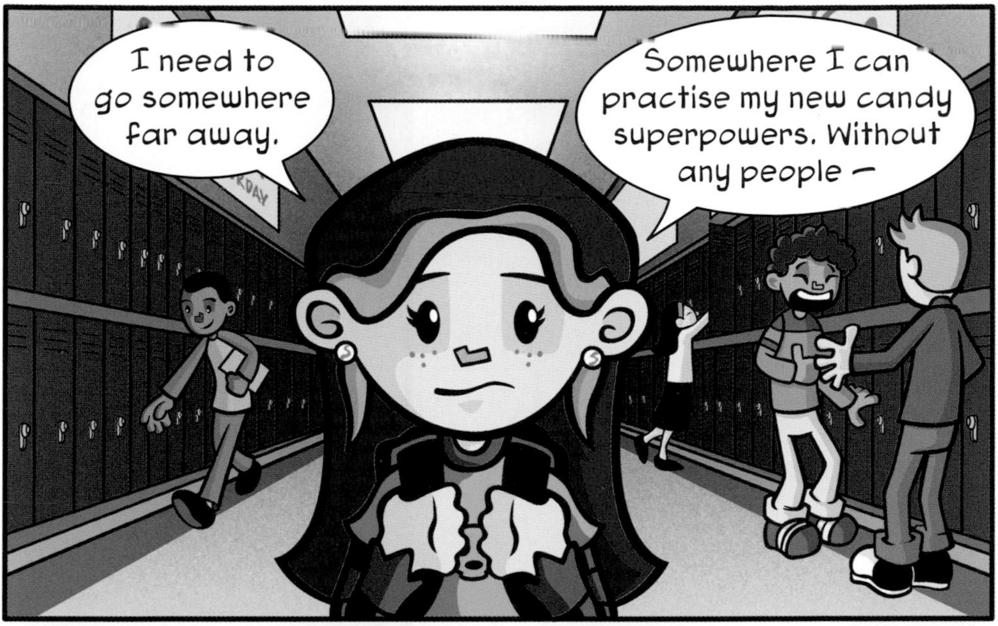
I need to go somewhere far away.
Somewhere I can practise my new candy superpowers. Without any people –

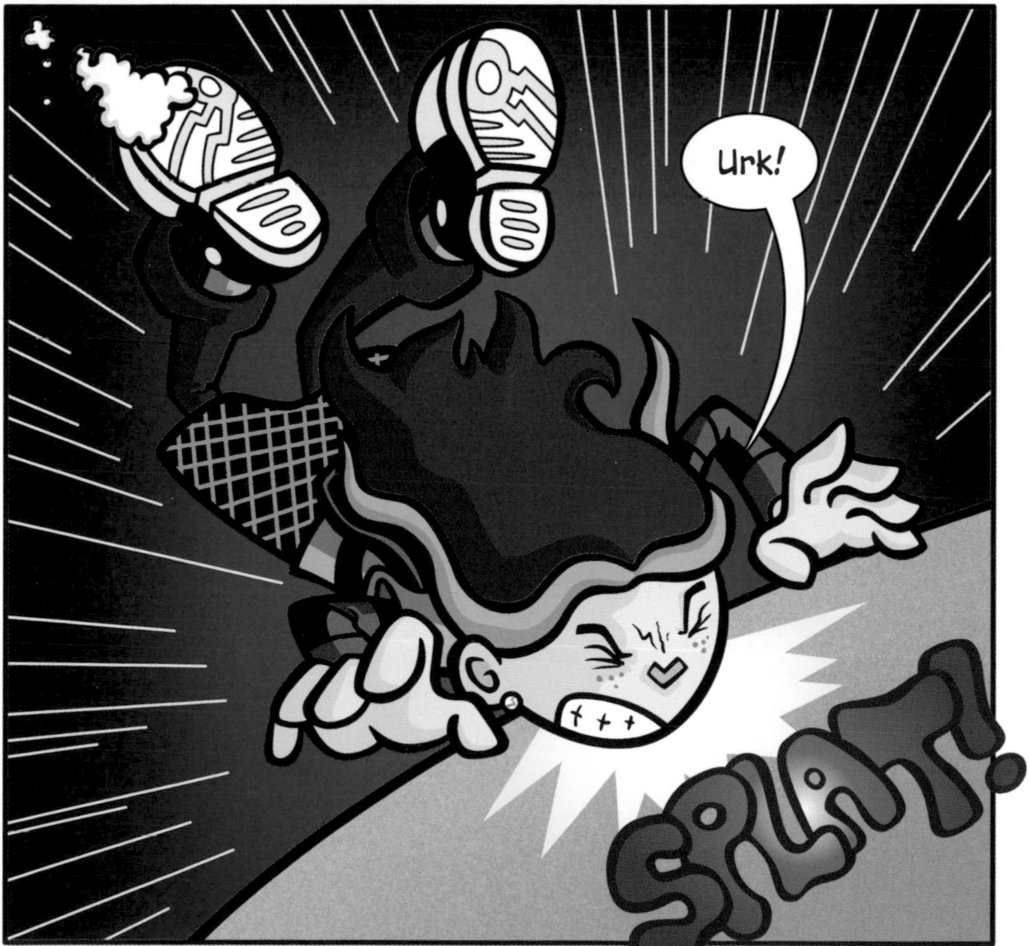
Urk!
SPLAT!

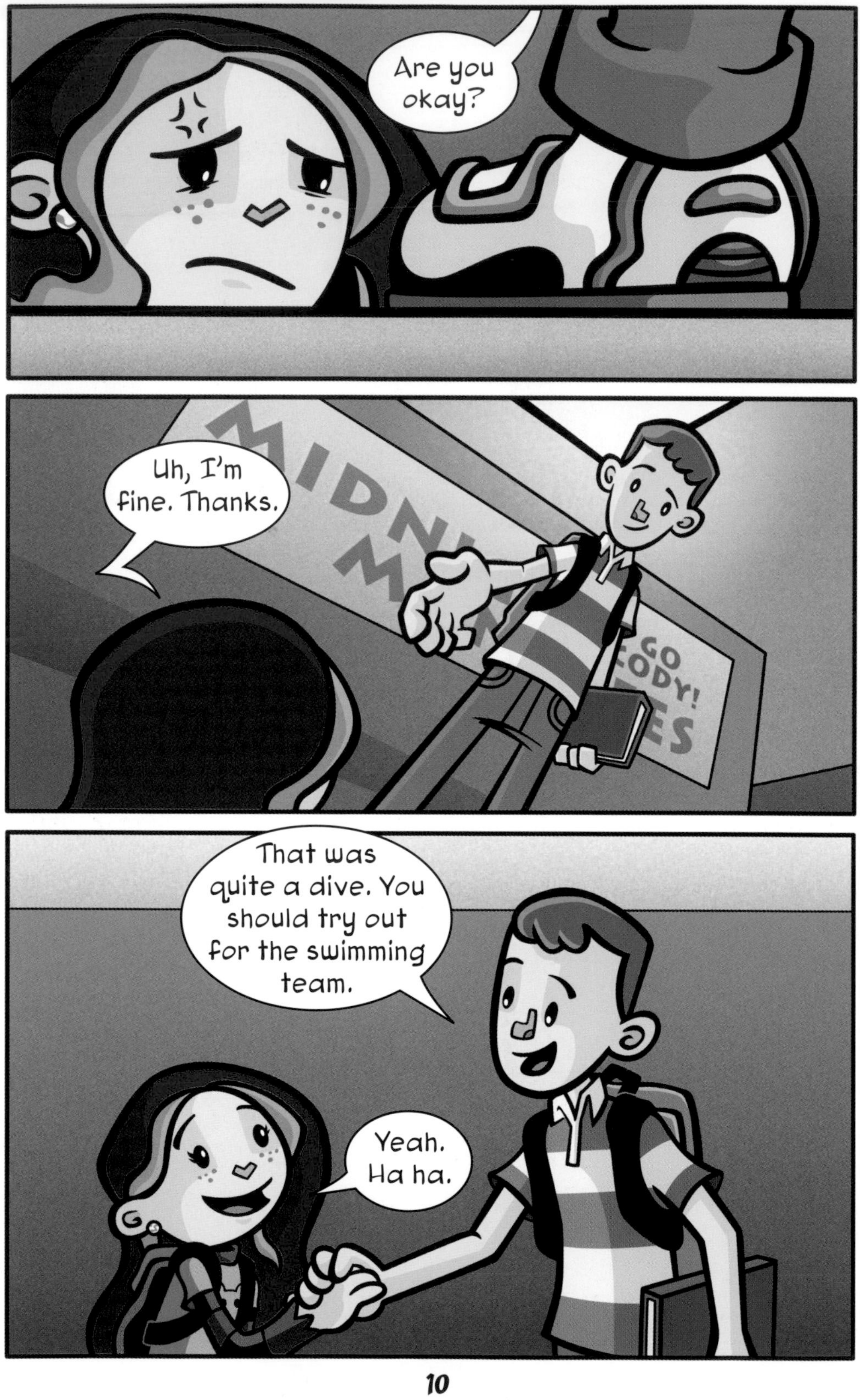
Are you okay?
Uh, I'm fine. Thanks.
That was quite a dive. You should try out for the swimming team.
Yeah. Ha ha.

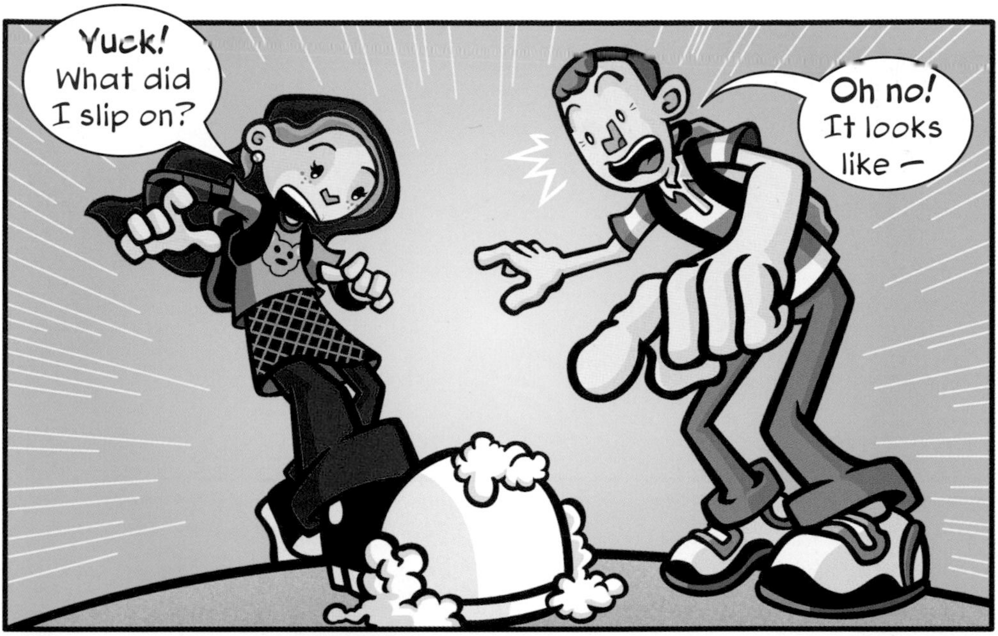
Yuck! What did I slip on?
Oh no! It looks like —

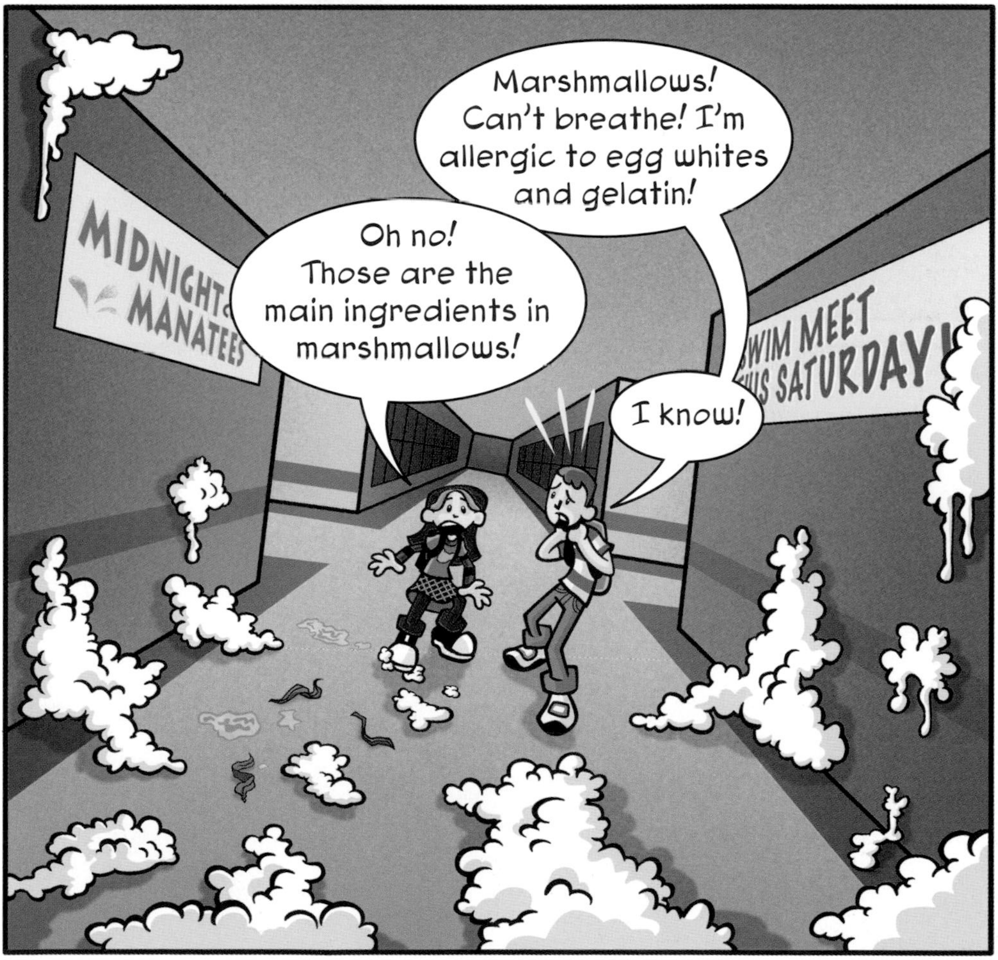
MIDNIGHT MANATEES
SWIM MEET THIS SATURDAY!
Marshmallows! Can't breathe! I'm allergic to egg whites and gelatin!
Oh no! Those are the main ingredients in marshmallows!
I know!

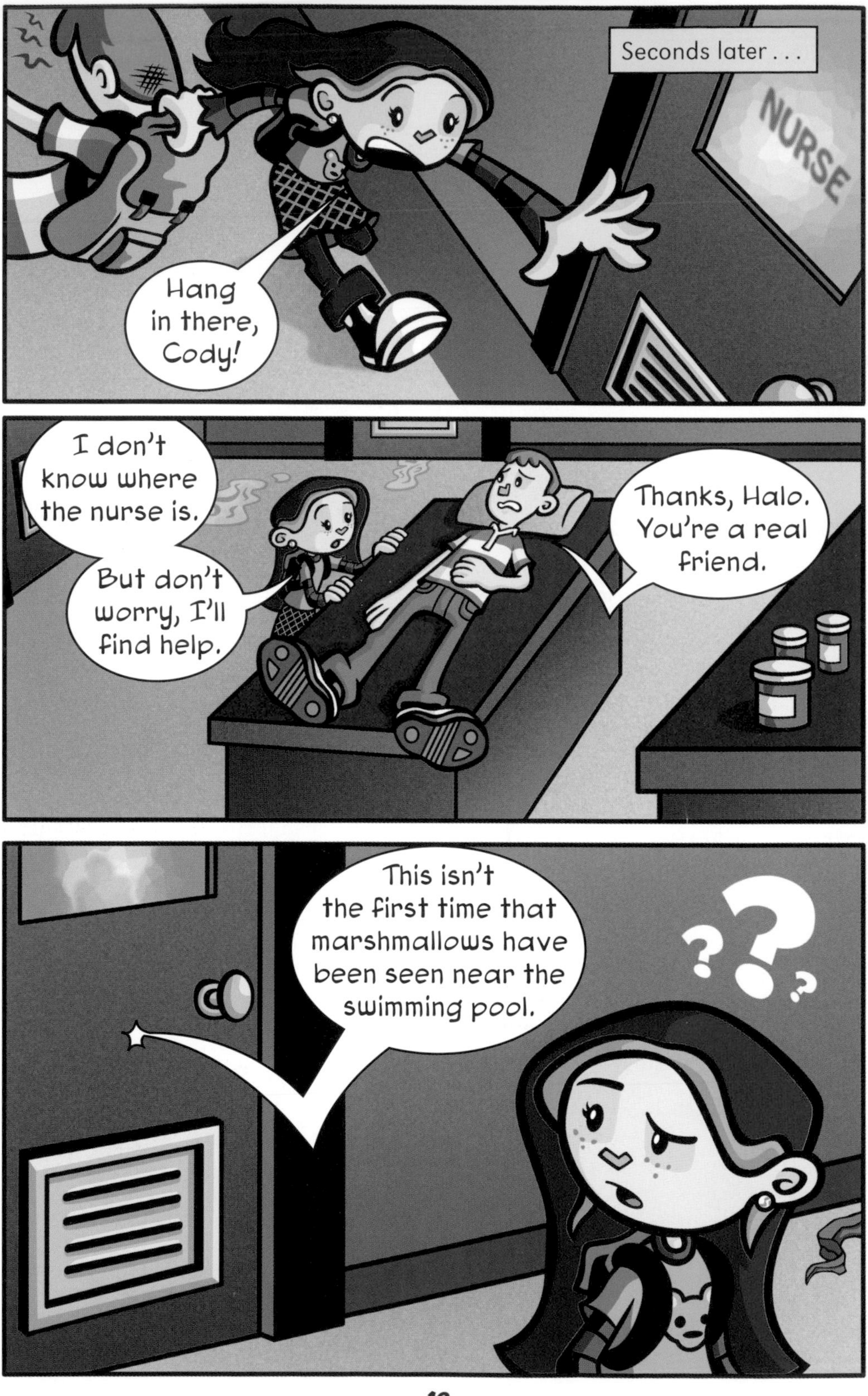
Seconds later . . .
NURSE
Hang in there, Cody!
I don't know where the nurse is.
But don't worry, I'll find help.
Thanks, Halo. You're a real friend.
This isn't the first time that marshmallows have been seen near the swimming pool.

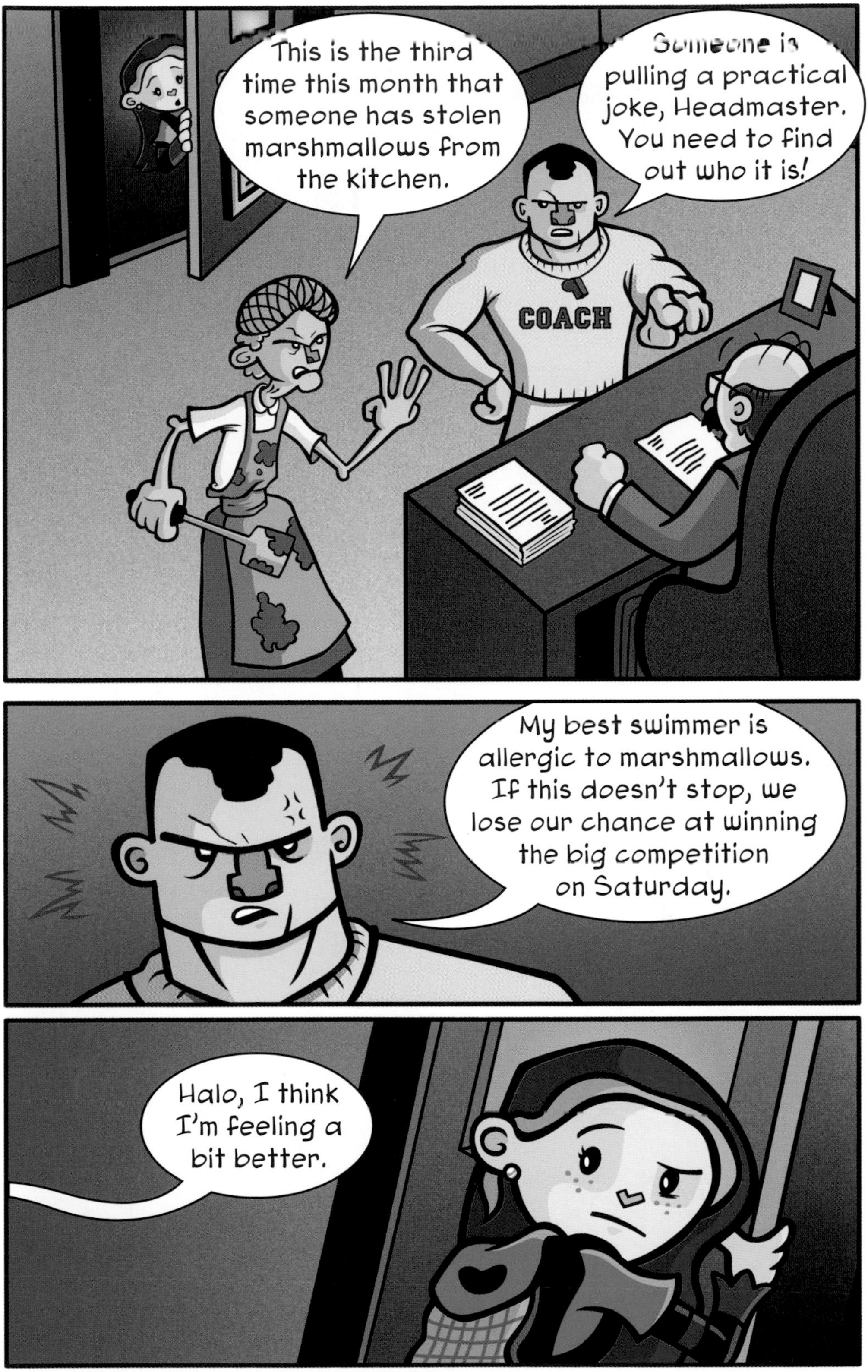
This is the third time this month that someone has stolen marshmallows from the kitchen.
Someone is pulling a practical joke, Headmaster. You need to find out who it is!
COACH
My best swimmer is allergic to marshmallows. If this doesn't stop, we lose our chance at winning the big competition on Saturday.
Halo, I think I'm feeling a bit better.

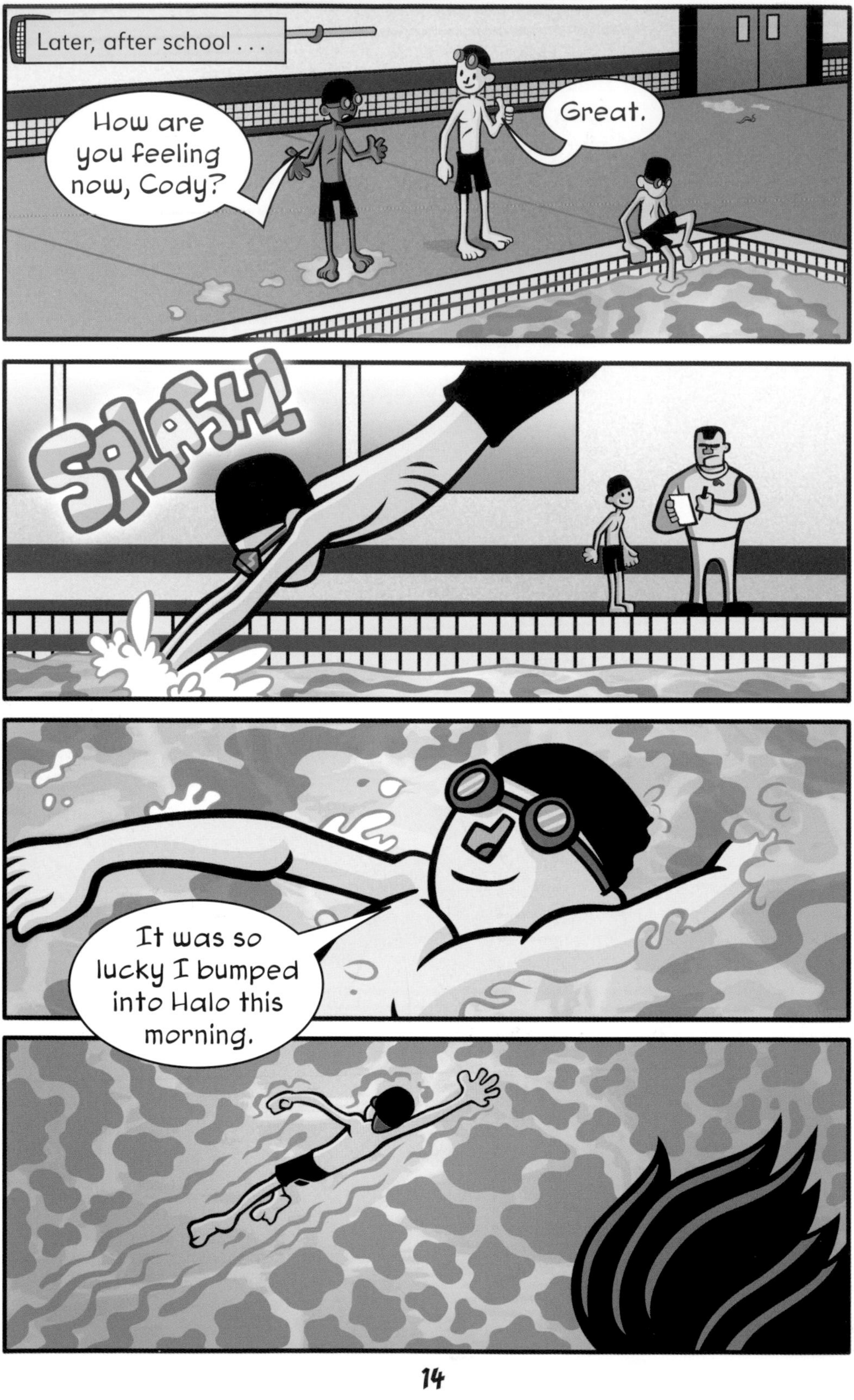
Later, after school . . .
How are you feeling now, Cody?
Great.
SPLASH!
It was so lucky I bumped into Halo this morning.

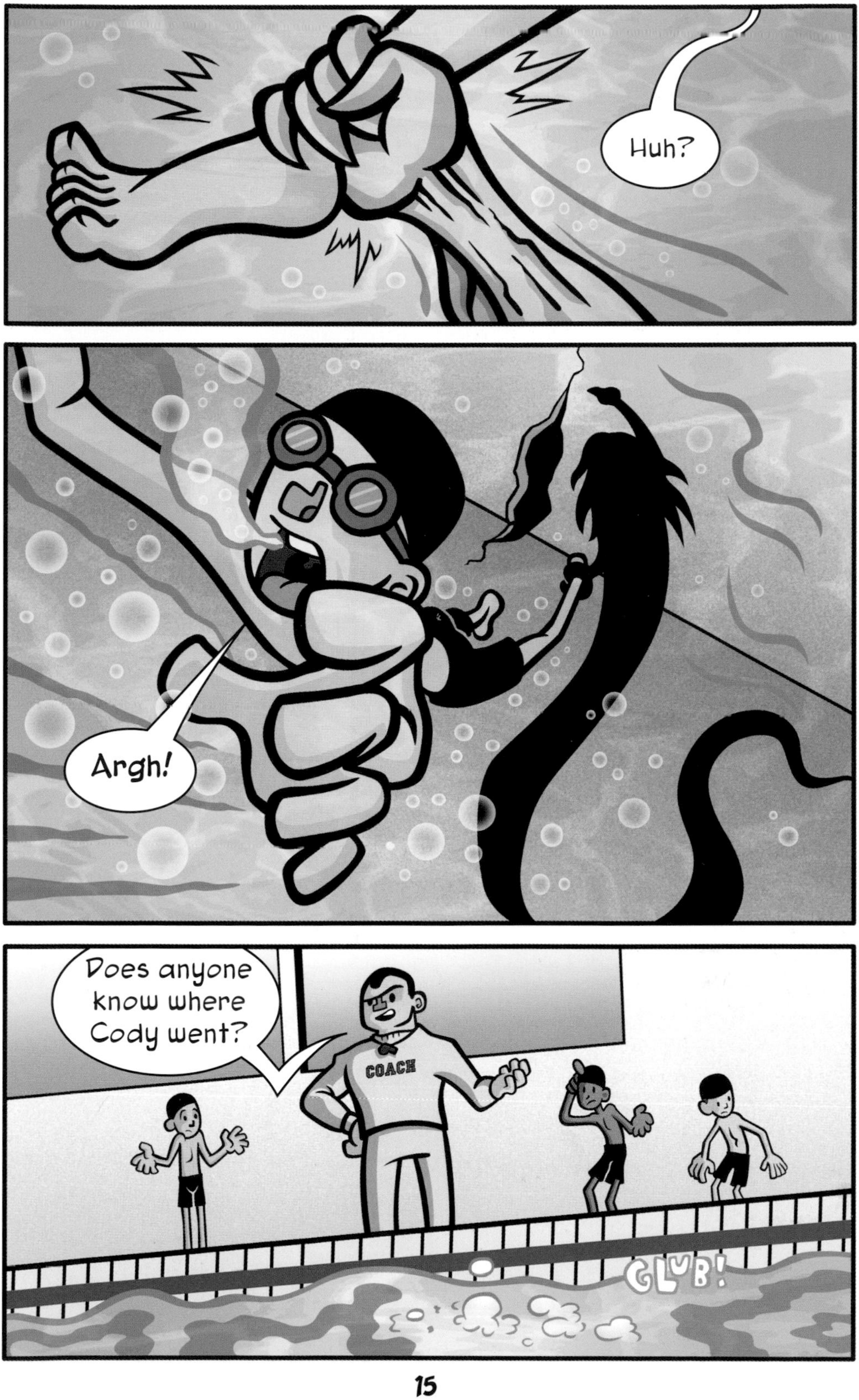
Huh?
Argh!
Does anyone know where Cody went?
GLUB!

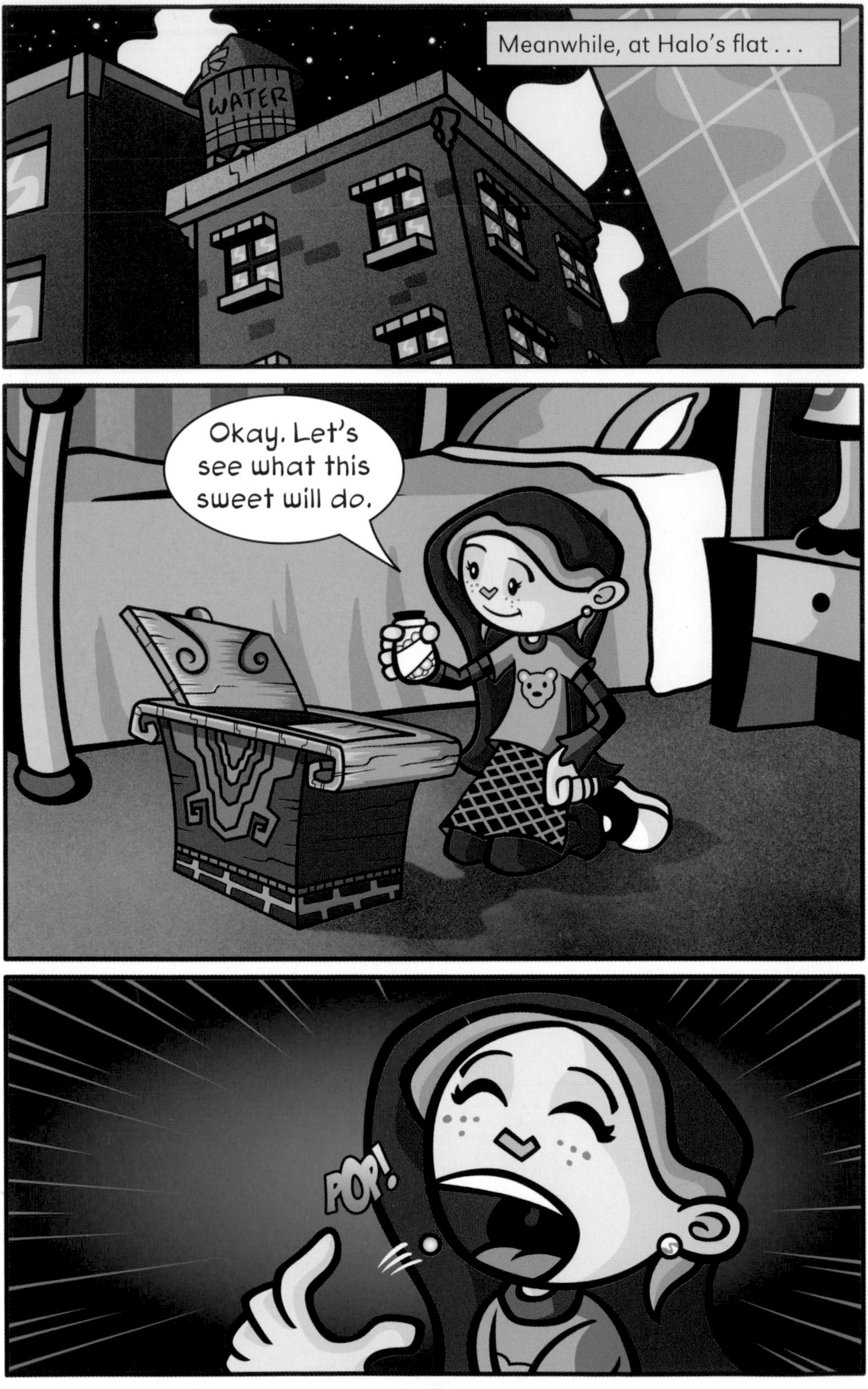
Meanwhile, at Halo's flat . . .
WATER
Okay. Let's see what this sweet will do.
POP!

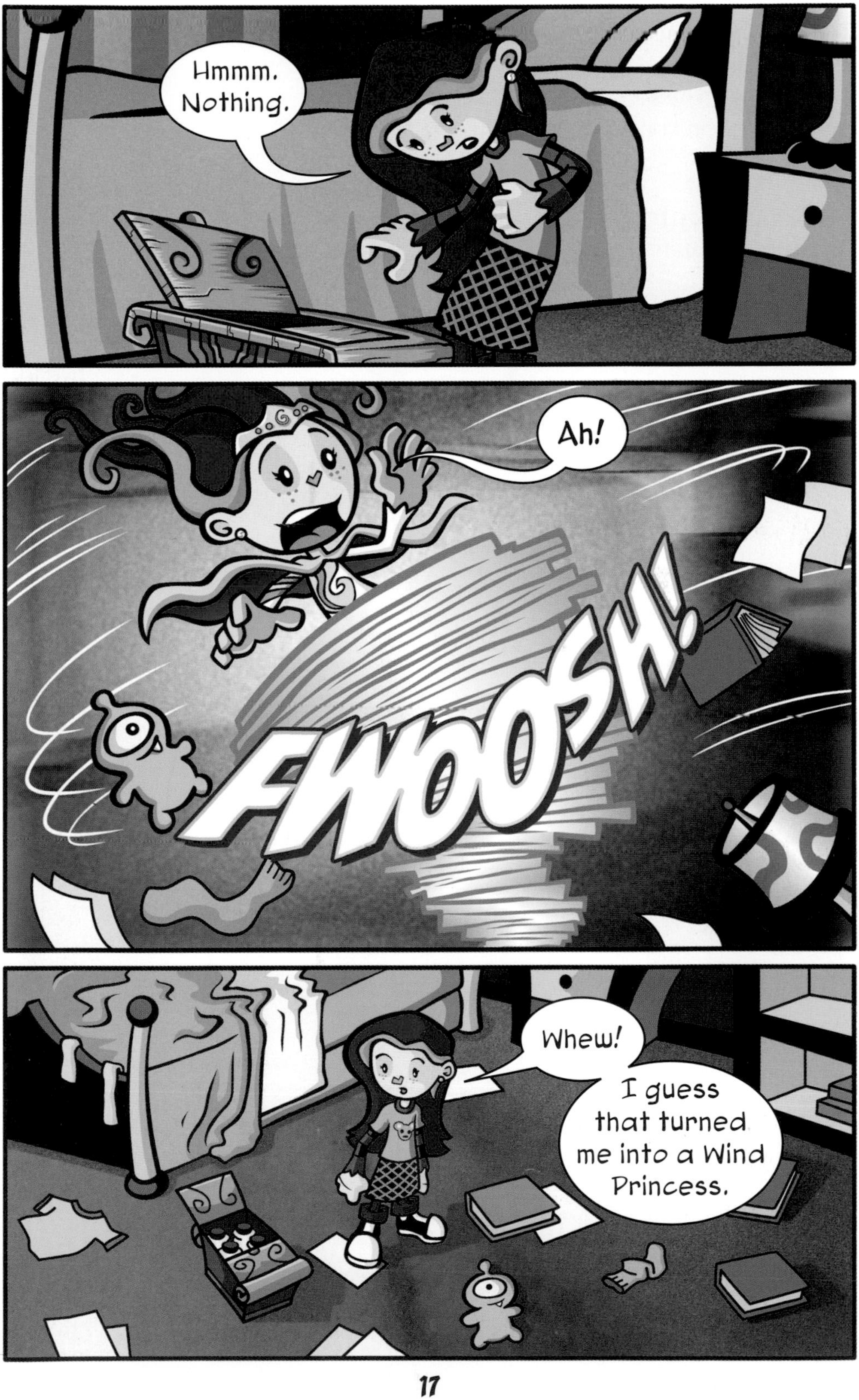
Hmmm. Nothing.
Ah!
FWOOSH!
Whew!
I guess that turned me into a Wind Princess.

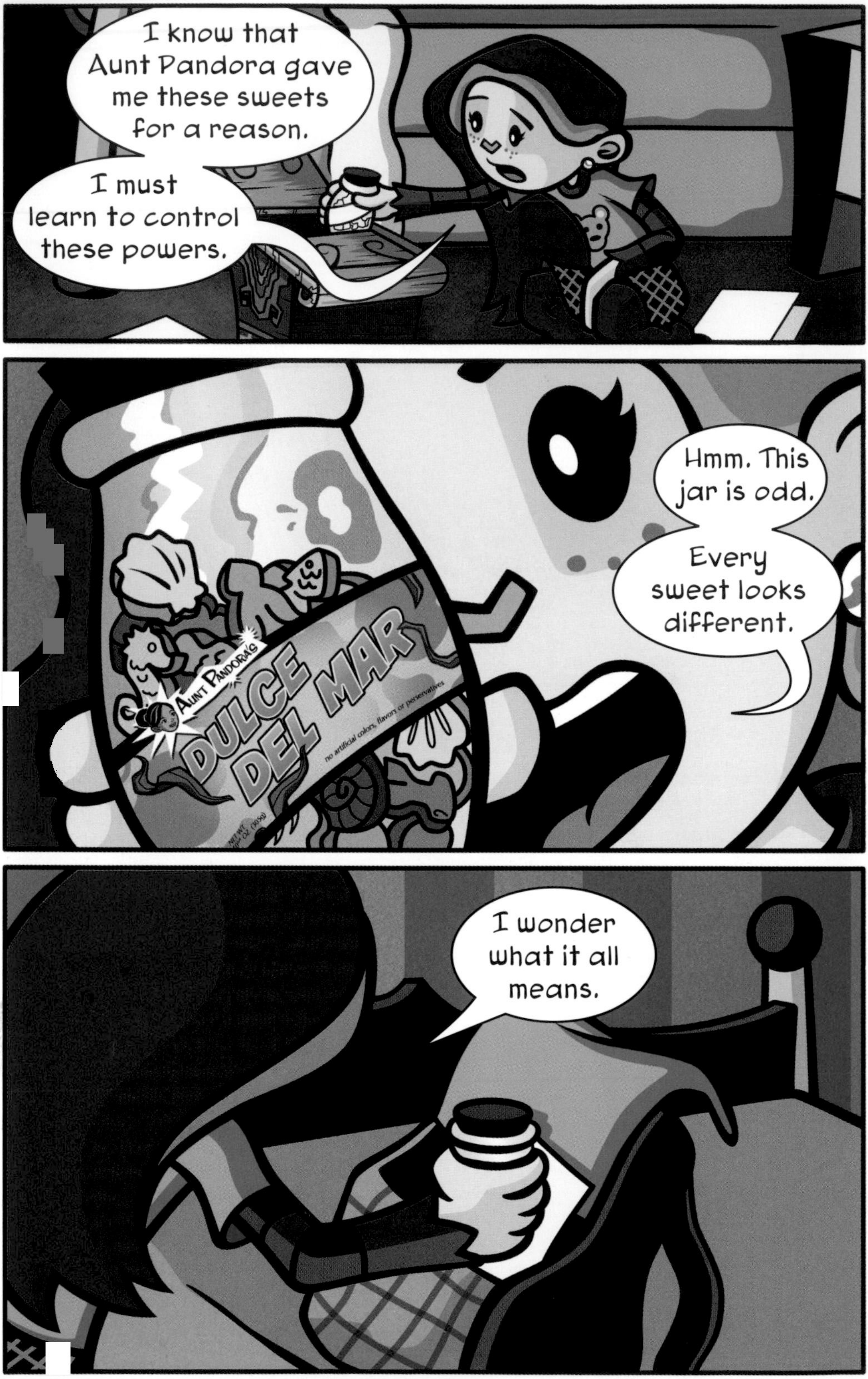
I know that Aunt Pandora gave me these sweets for a reason.
I must learn to control these powers.
Hmm. This jar is odd.
Every sweet looks different.
AUNT PANDORA'S
DULCE DEL MAR
no artificial colors, flavors or perservatives
I wonder what it all means.

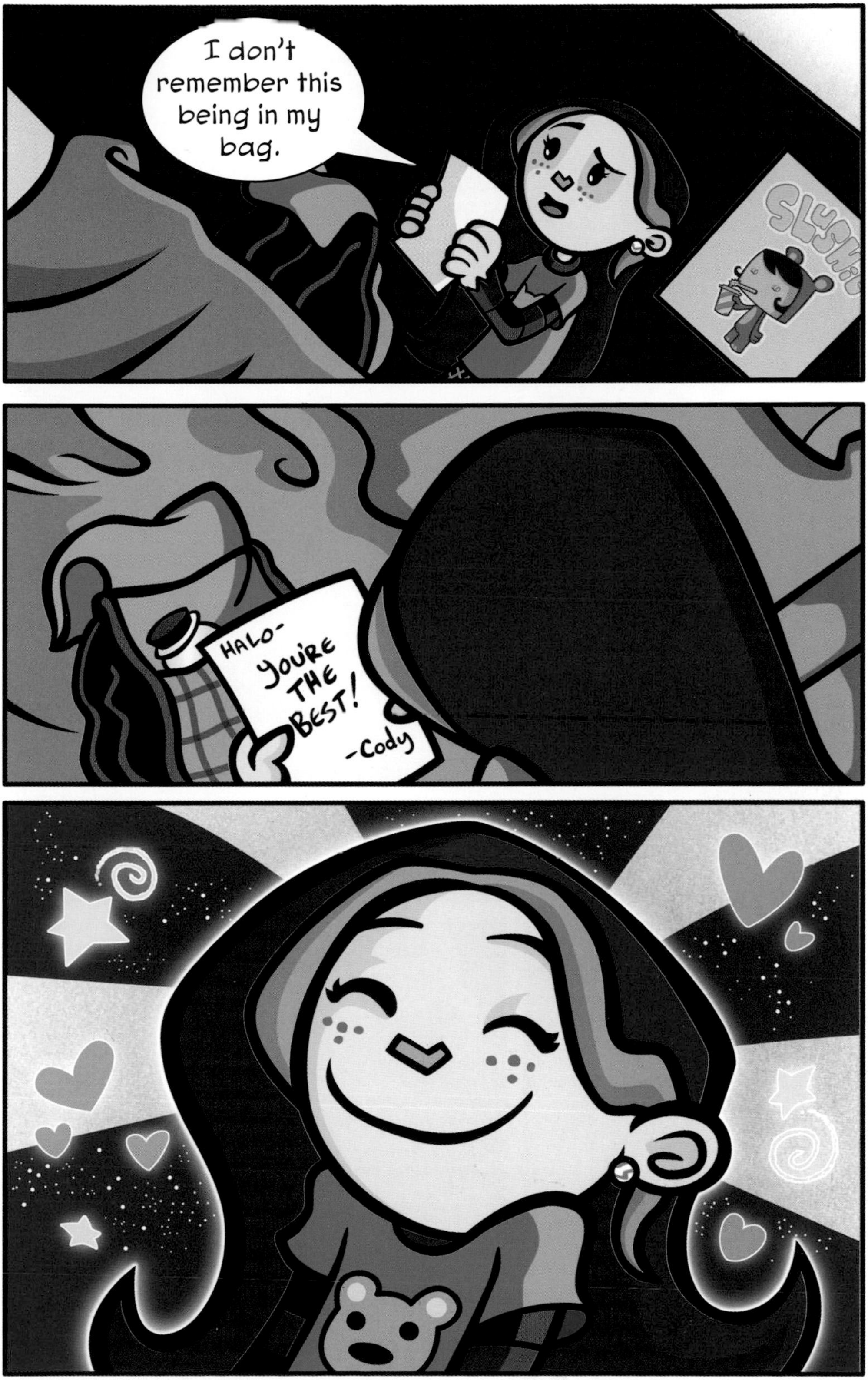
I don't remember this being in my bag.
SLUSH
HALO- YOU'RE THE BEST! -Cody

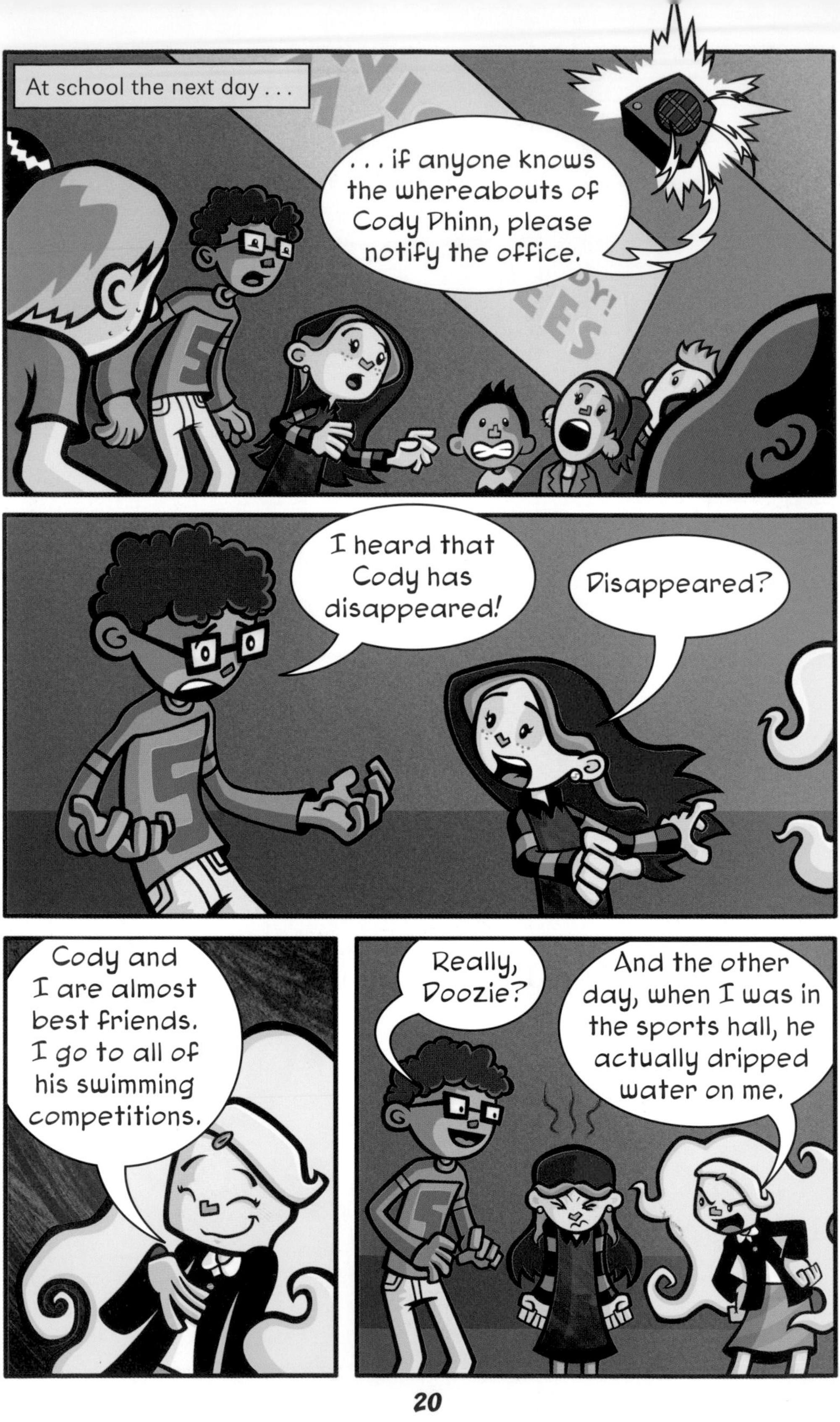
At school the next day . . .
. . . if anyone knows the whereabouts of Cody Phinn, please notify the office.
I heard that Cody has disappeared!
Disappeared?
Cody and I are almost best friends. I go to all of his swimming competitions.
Really, Doozie?
And the other day, when I was in the sports hall, he actually dripped water on me.

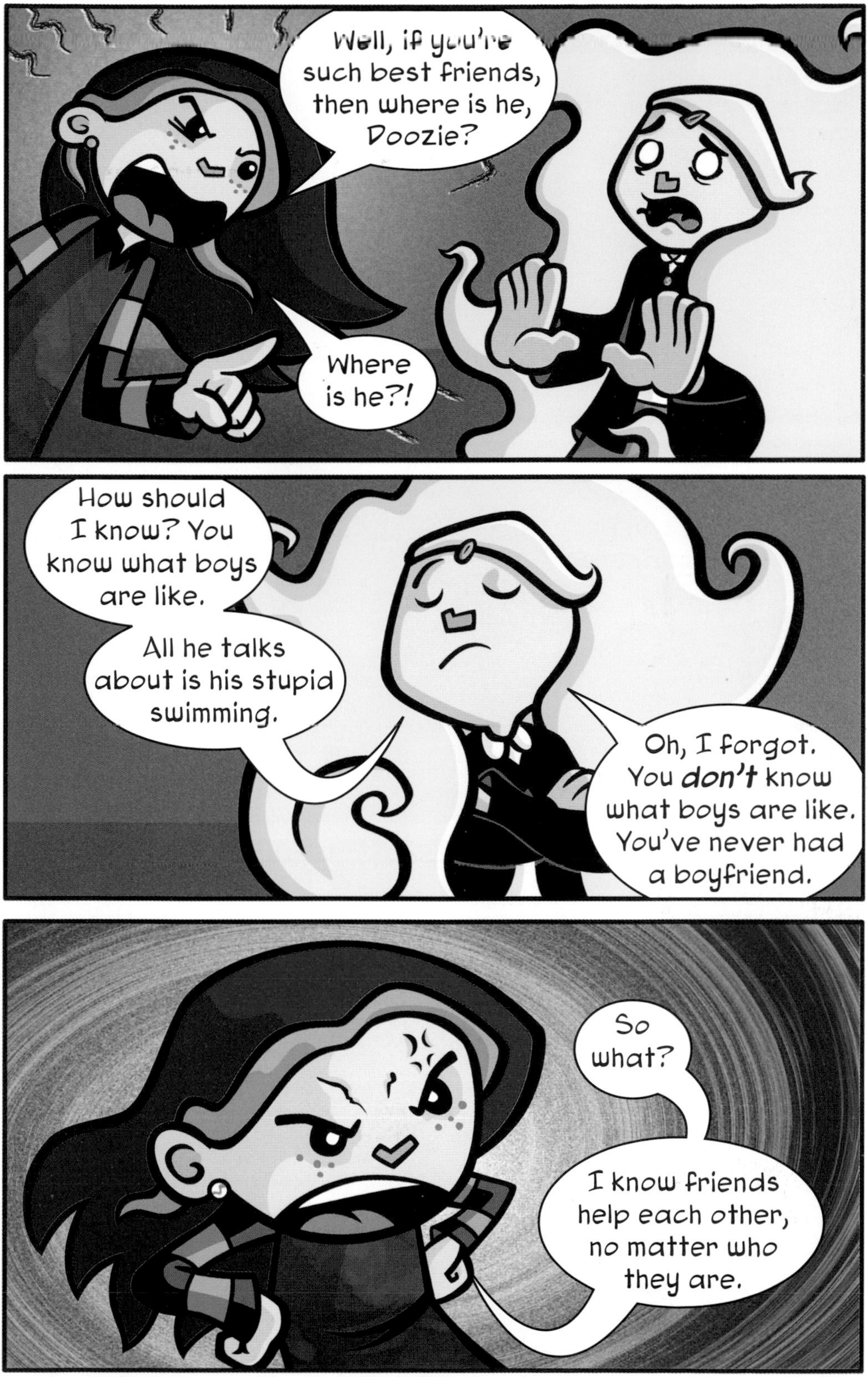
Well, if you're such best friends, then where is he, Doozie?
Where is he?!
How should I know? You know what boys are like.
All he talks about is his stupid swimming.
Oh, I forgot. You *don't* know what boys are like. You've never had a boyfriend.
So what?
I know friends help each other, no matter who they are.

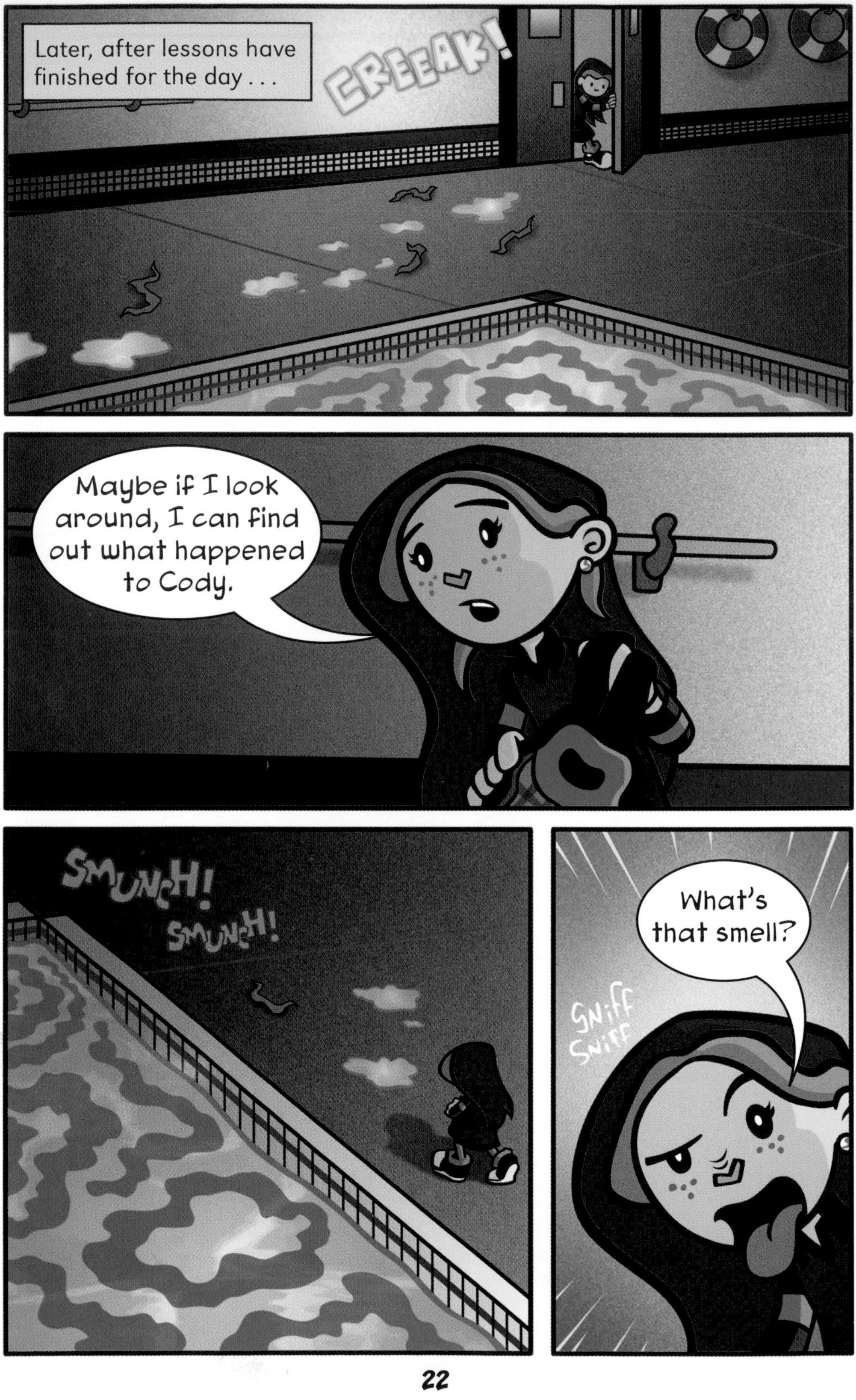
Later, after lessons have finished for the day . . .
CREEAK!
Maybe if I look around, I can find out what happened to Cody.
SMUNCH!
SMUNCH!
SNiff SNiff
What's that smell?

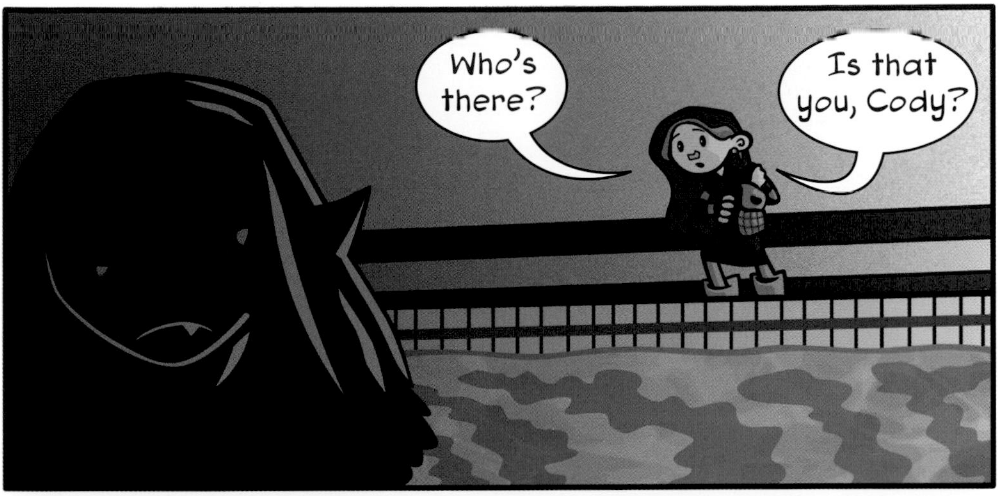
Who's there?
Is that you, Cody?

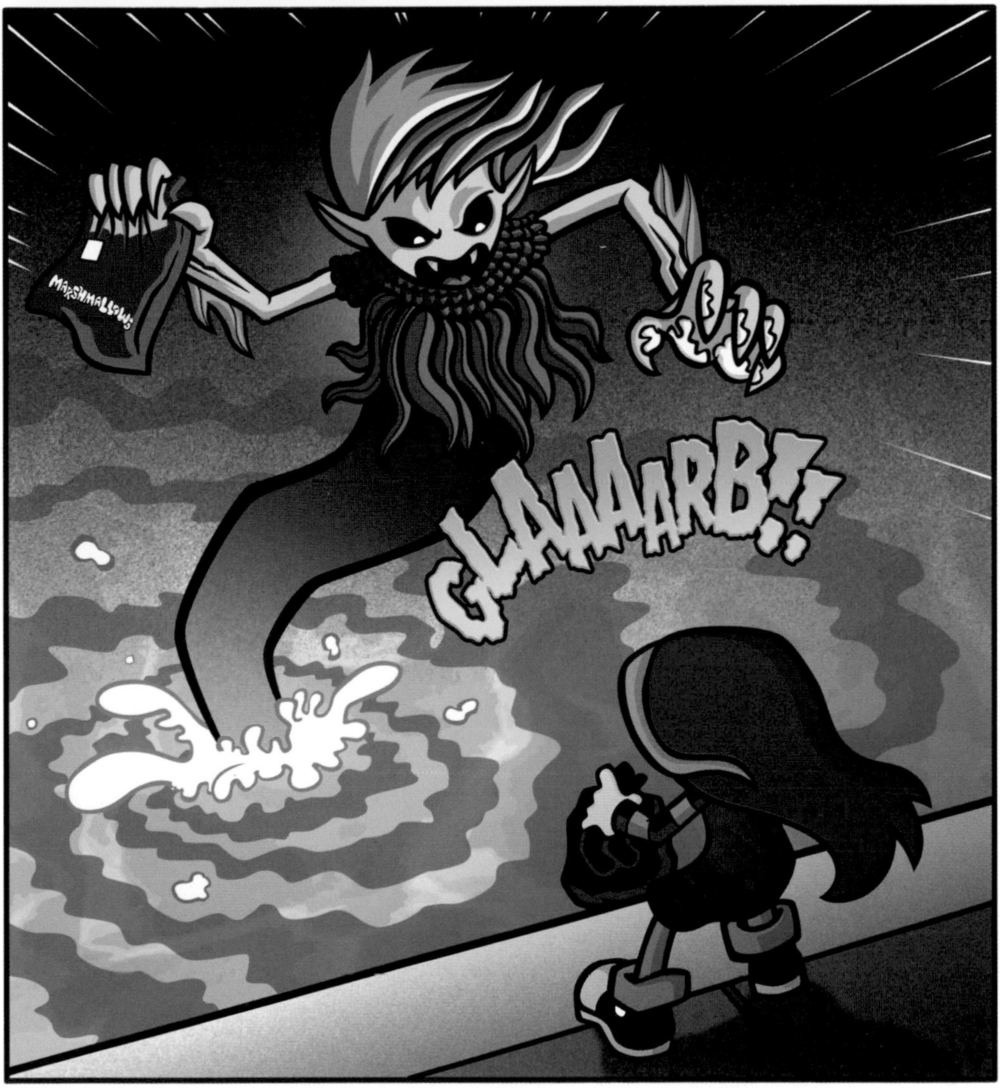
MARSHMALLOWS
GLAAAARB!!

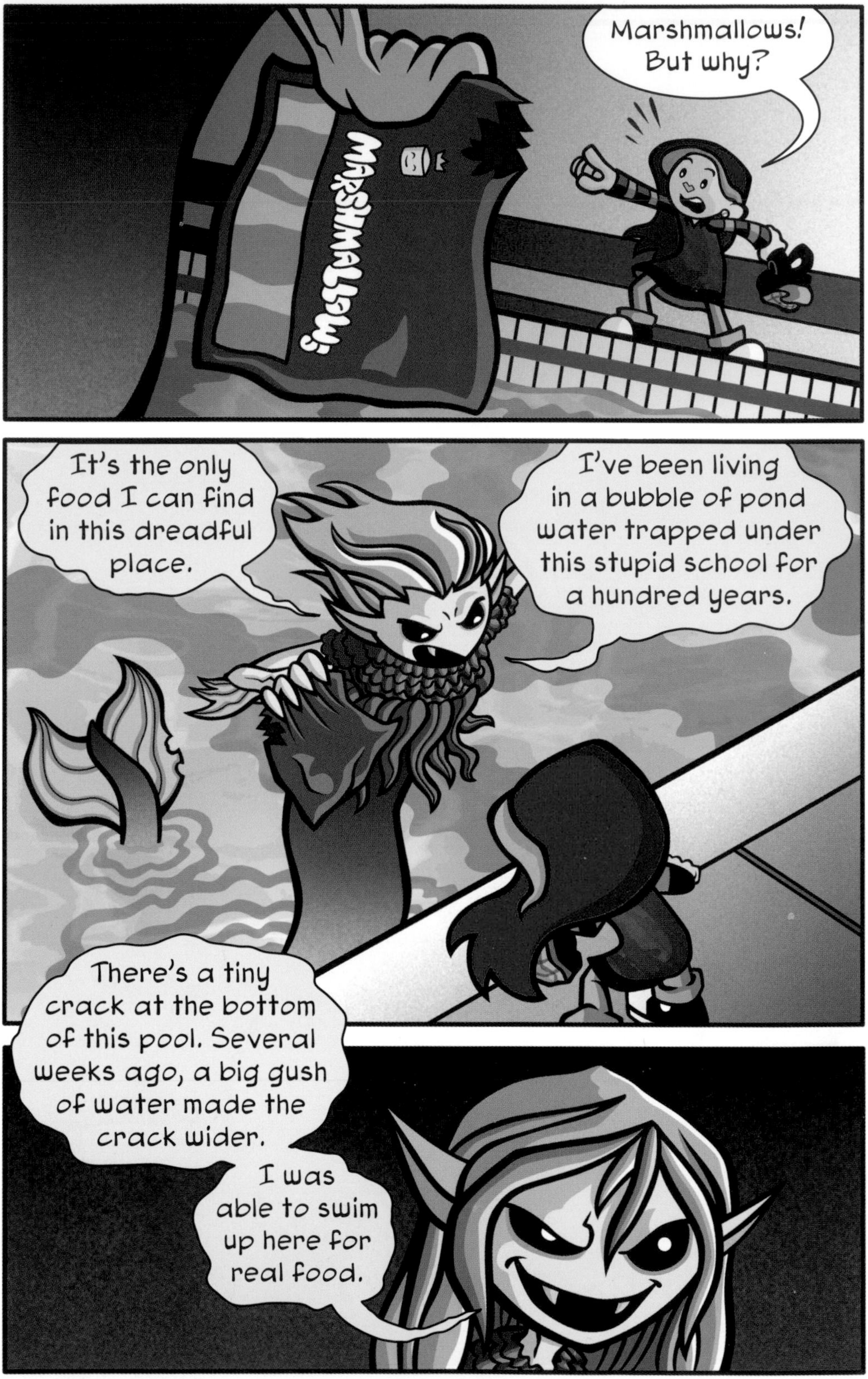
Marshmallows! But why?
MARSHMALLOWS!
It's the only food I can find in this dreadful place.
I've been living in a bubble of pond water trapped under this stupid school for a hundred years.
There's a tiny crack at the bottom of this pool. Several weeks ago, a big gush of water made the crack wider.
I was able to swim up here for real food.

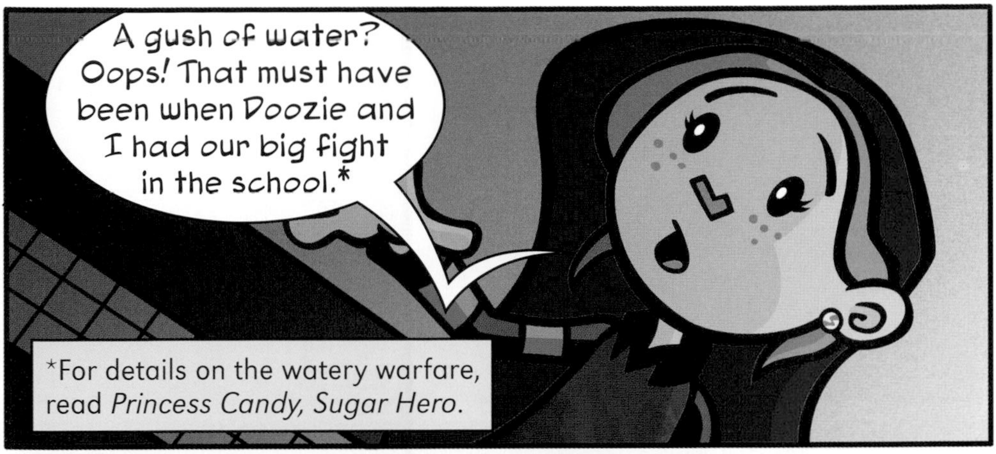
A gush of water? Oops! That must have been when Doozie and I had our big fight in the school.*
*For details on the watery warfare, read *Princess Candy, Sugar Hero*.

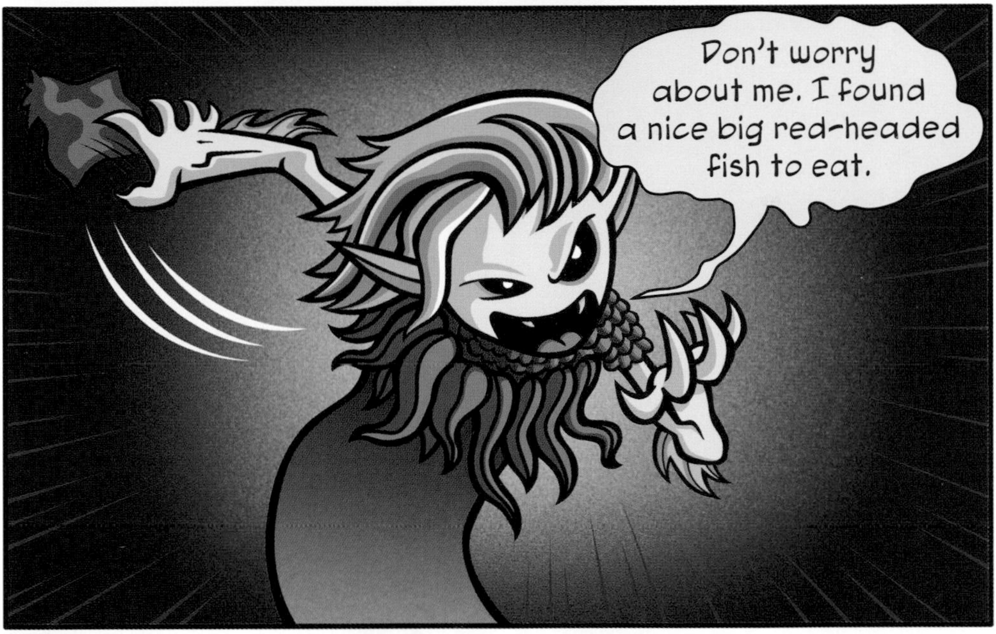
Don't worry about me. I found a nice big red-headed fish to eat.

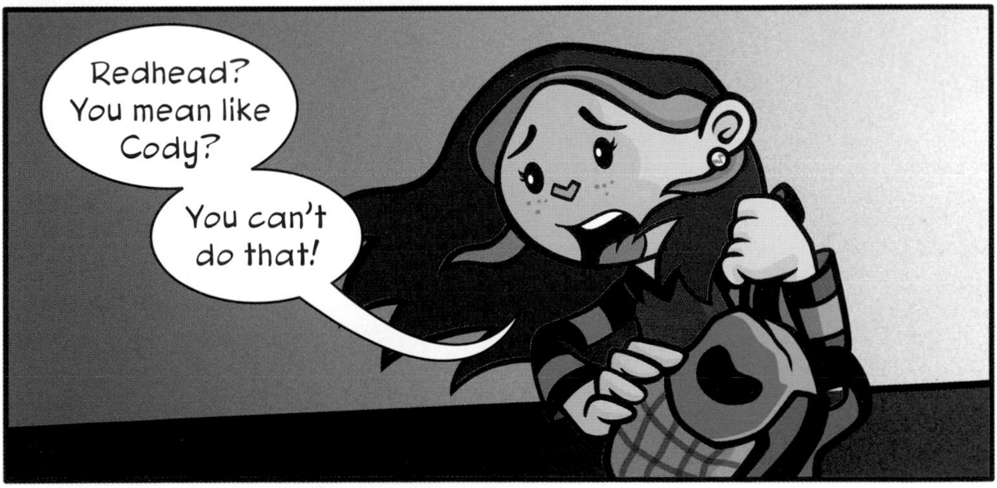
Redhead? You mean like Cody?
You can't do that!

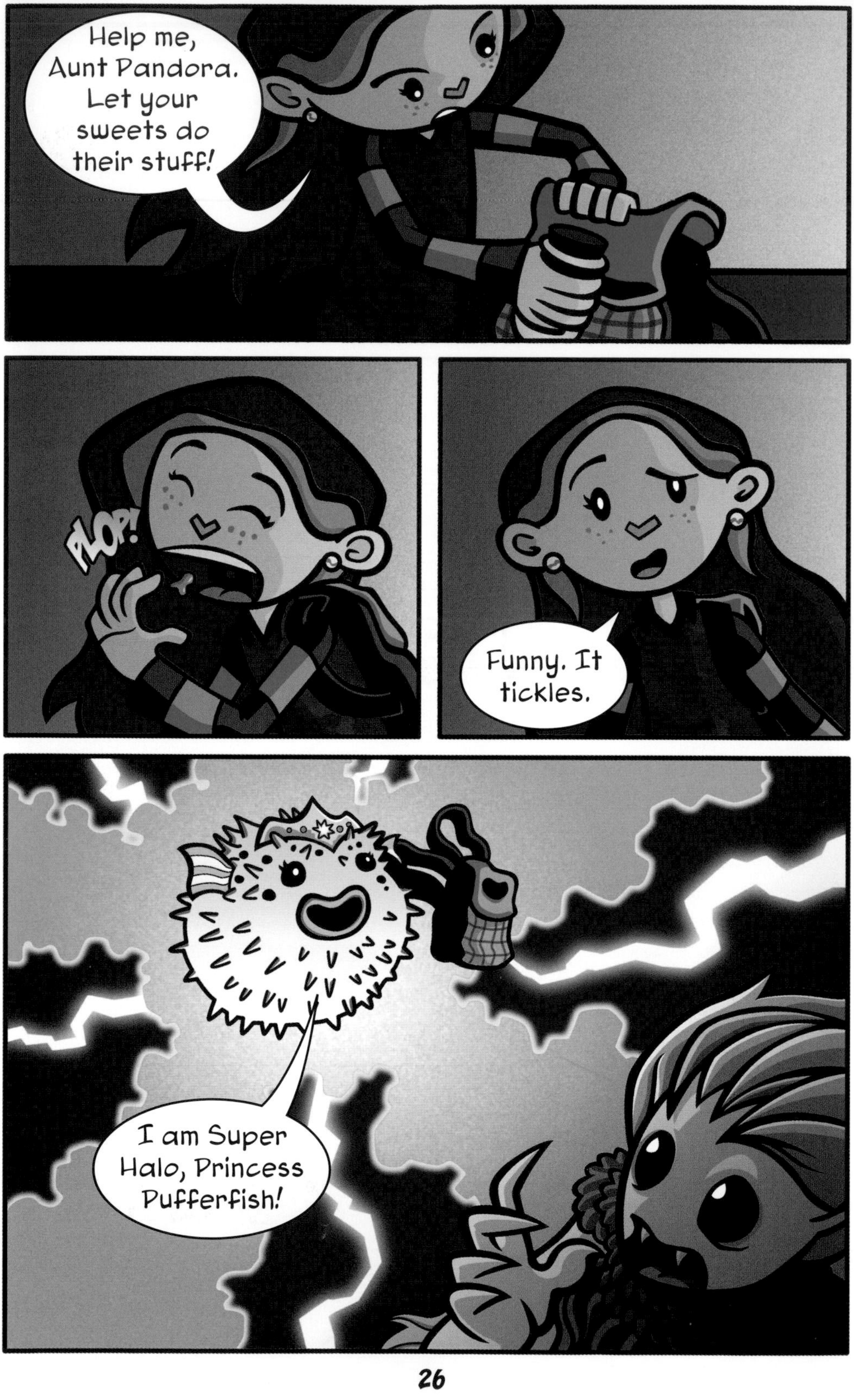
Help me, Aunt Pandora. Let your sweets do their stuff!
PLOP!
Funny. It tickles.
I am Super Halo, Princess Pufferfish!

Okay, so it's a funny name. It's still an amazing power!

Maybe you should go on a diet!

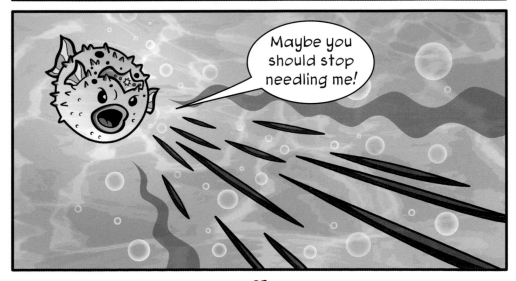

Maybe you should stop needling me!

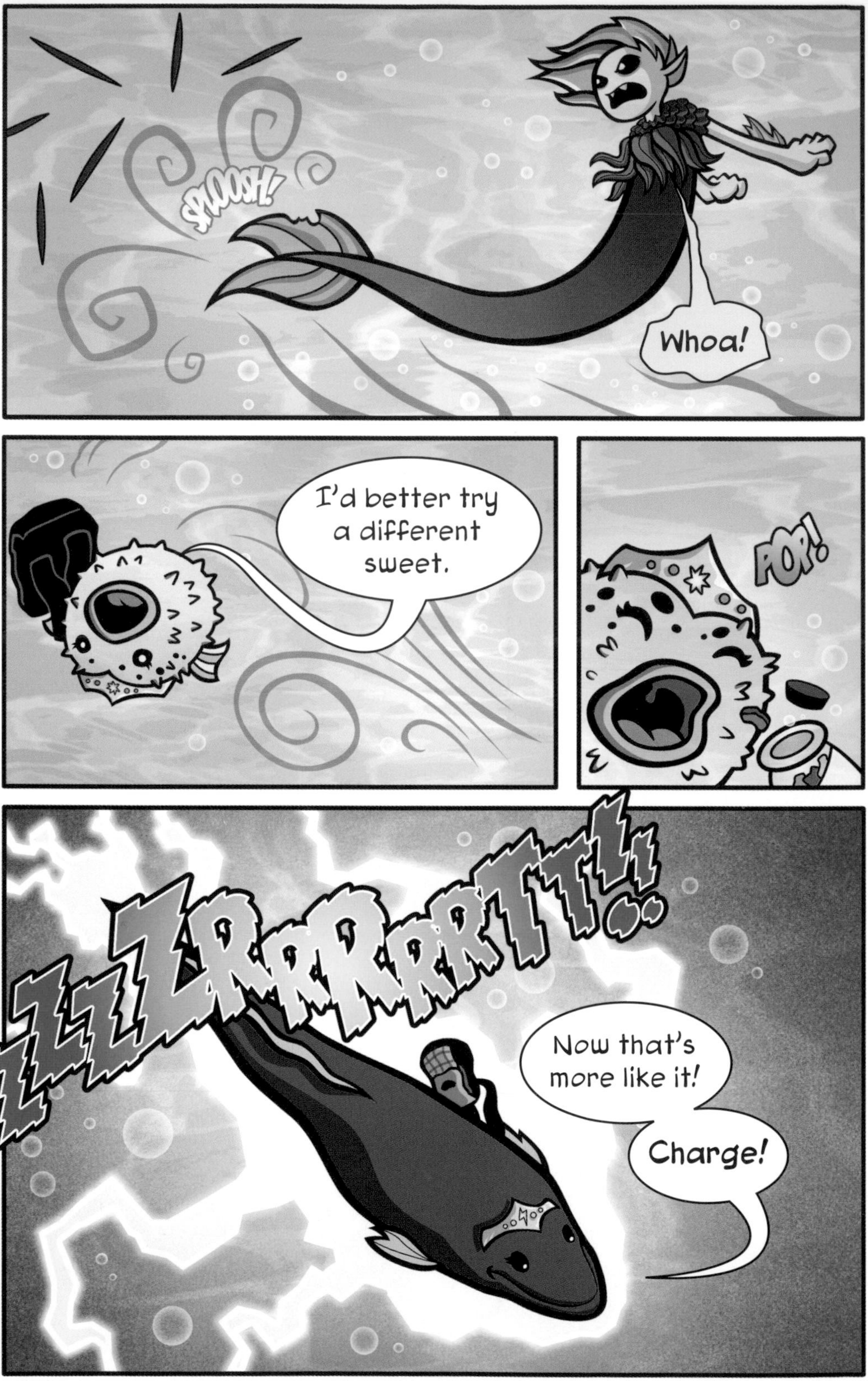
SPLOOSH!
Whoa!
I'd better try a different sweet.
POP!
ZZZZRRRRRRTTT!!
Now that's more like it!
Charge!

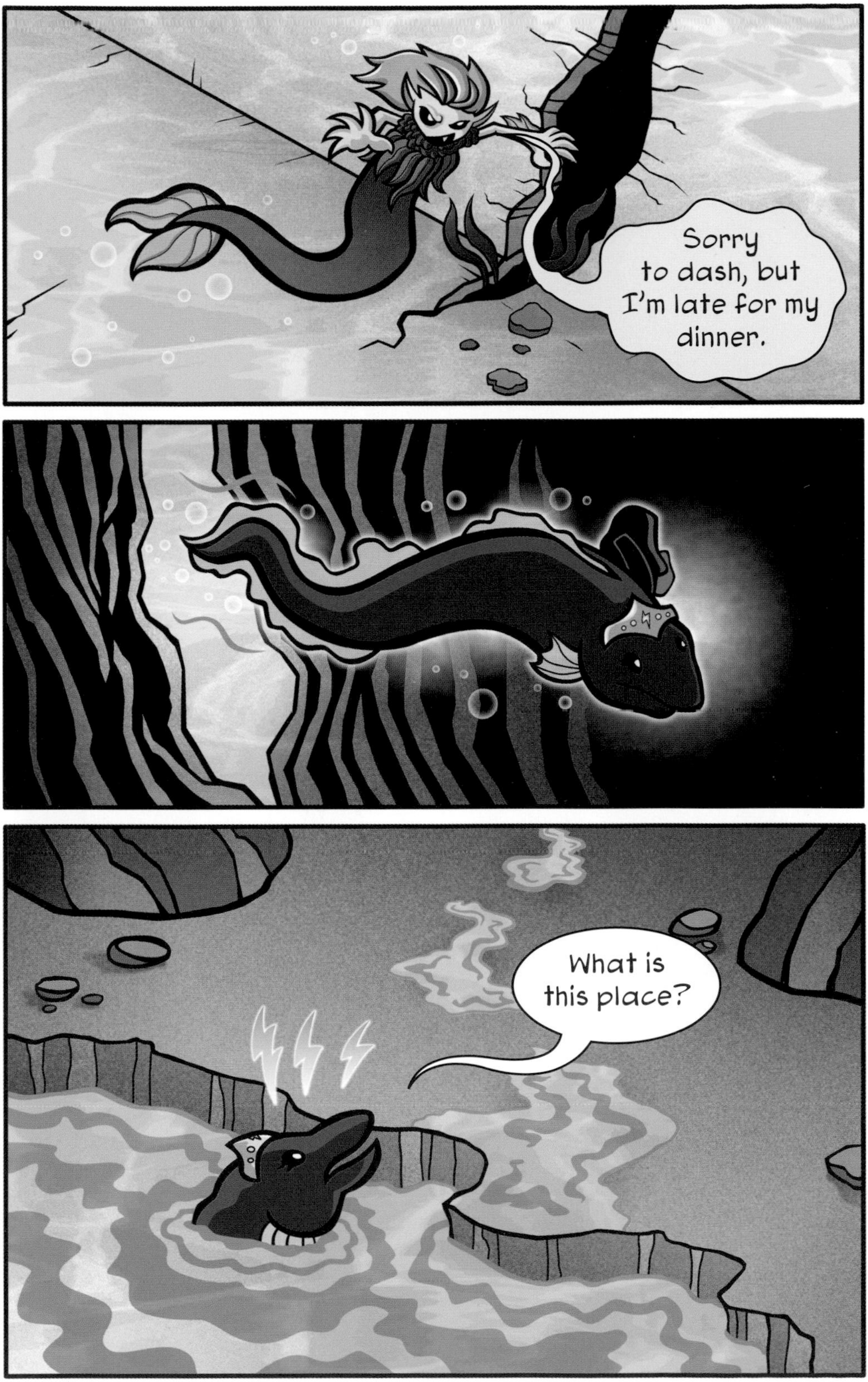
Sorry to dash, but I'm late for my dinner.
What is this place?

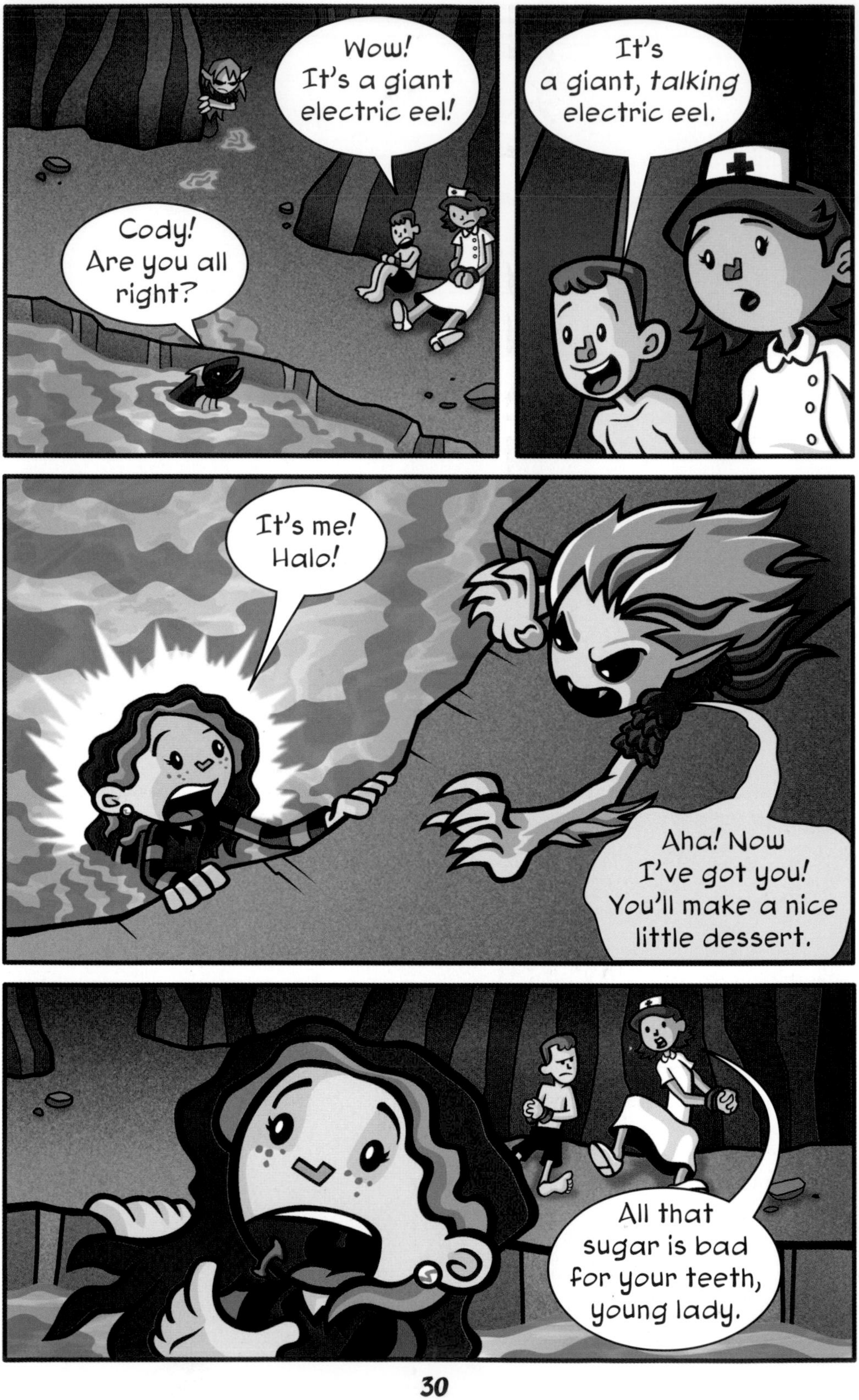
Wow! It's a giant electric eel!
Cody! Are you all right?
It's a giant, *talking* electric eel.
It's me! Halo!
Aha! Now I've got you! You'll make a nice little dessert.
All that sugar is bad for your teeth, young lady.

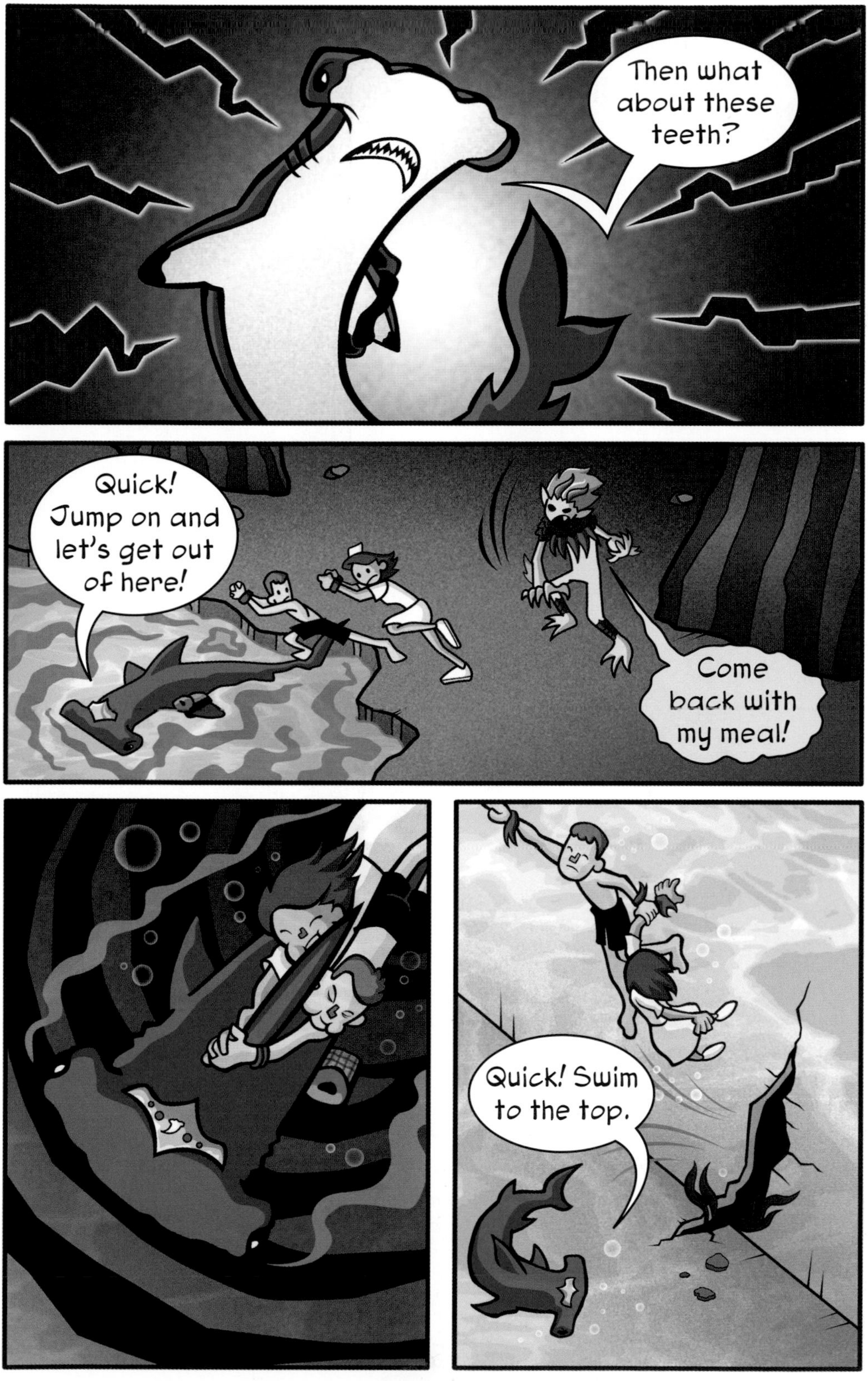
Then what about these teeth?
Quick! Jump on and let's get out of here!
Come back with my meal!
Quick! Swim to the top.

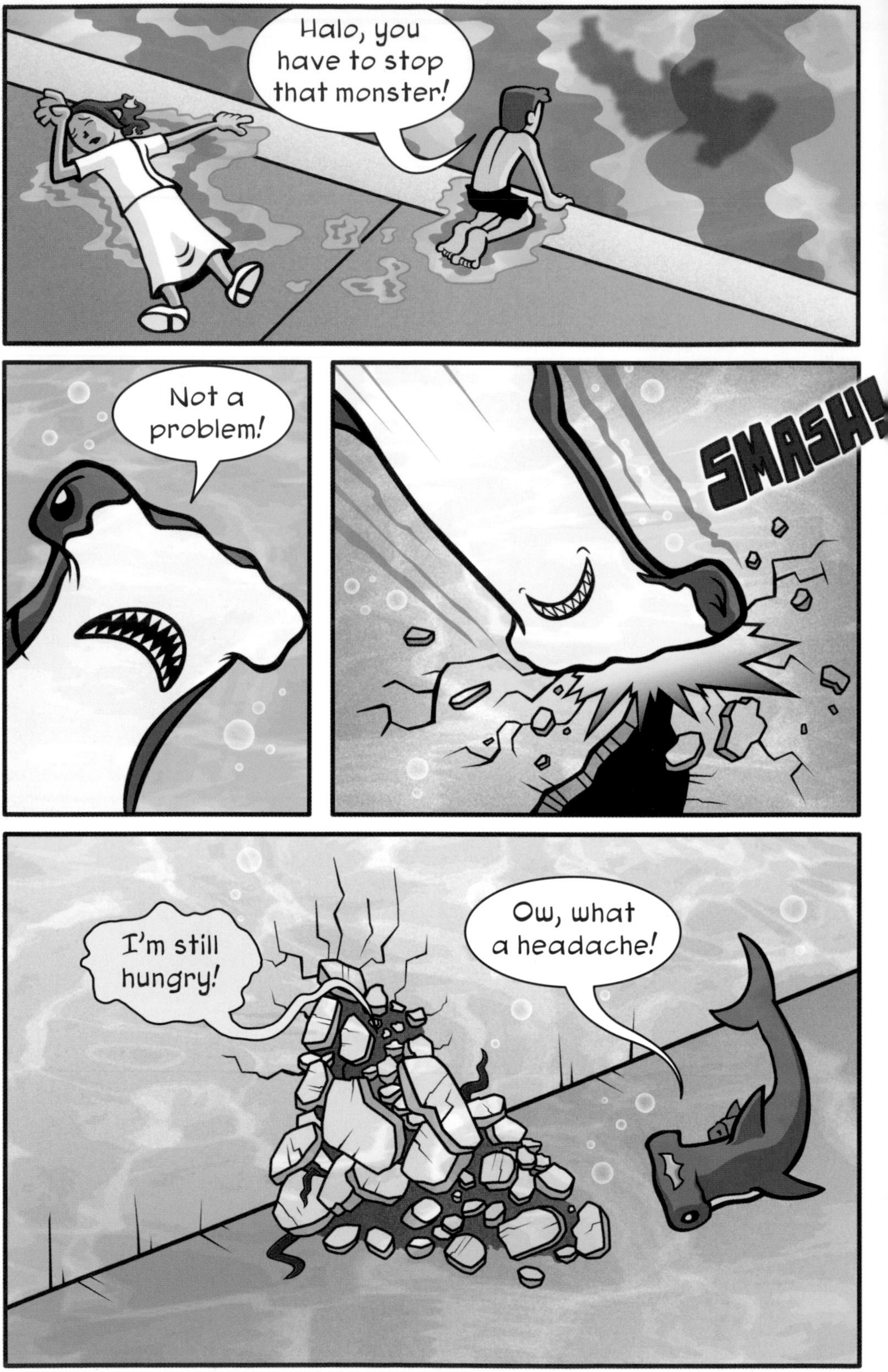
Halo, you have to stop that monster!
Not a problem!
SMASH!
I'm still hungry!
Ow, what a headache!

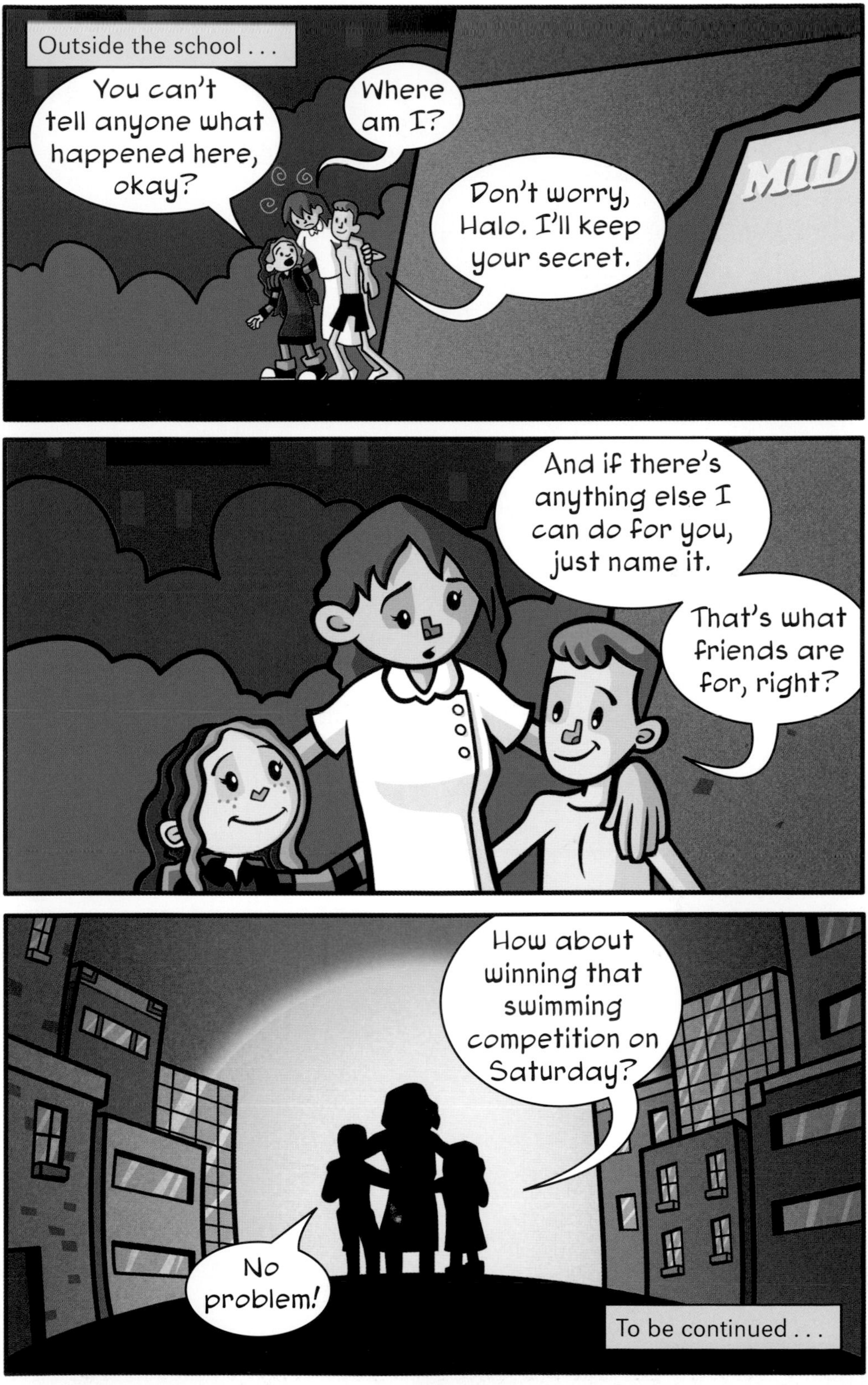
Outside the school . . .
You can't tell anyone what happened here, okay?
Where am I?
MID
Don't worry, Halo. I'll keep your secret.
And if there's anything else I can do for you, just name it.
That's what friends are for, right?
How about winning that swimming competition on Saturday?
No problem!
To be continued . . .

About The Author

Michael Dahl is the author of more than 200 books for children and young adults. He has won the AEP Distinguished Achievement Award three times for his non-fiction. His Finnegan Zwake mystery series was shortlisted twice by the Anthony and Agatha awards. He has also written the Library of Doom series and the Dragonblood books. He speaks at US conferences about graphic novels and high-interest books for boys.

About The Illustrator

Jeff Crowther has been drawing comics for as long as he can remember. Since graduating from college, Jeff has worked on a variety of illustrations for clients including Disney, Adventures Magazine and Boy's Life Magazine. He also wrote and illustrated the webcomic Sketchbook and has self-published several mini-comics. Jeff lives in Ohio, USA, with his wife, Elizabeth, and their children, Jonas and Noelle.

GLOSSARY

allergic if you are allergic to something, it can cause a reaction, such as a rash, sneezing or sickness

dreadful very bad

gelatin a clear substance often used for making jelly or desserts

gush to flow quickly in large amounts

ingredients the items that something is made from

practical joke a prank intended to trick or embarrass someone

whereabouts roughly where someone or something is located

Marshmallow Mermaid

SUPER-VILLAIN

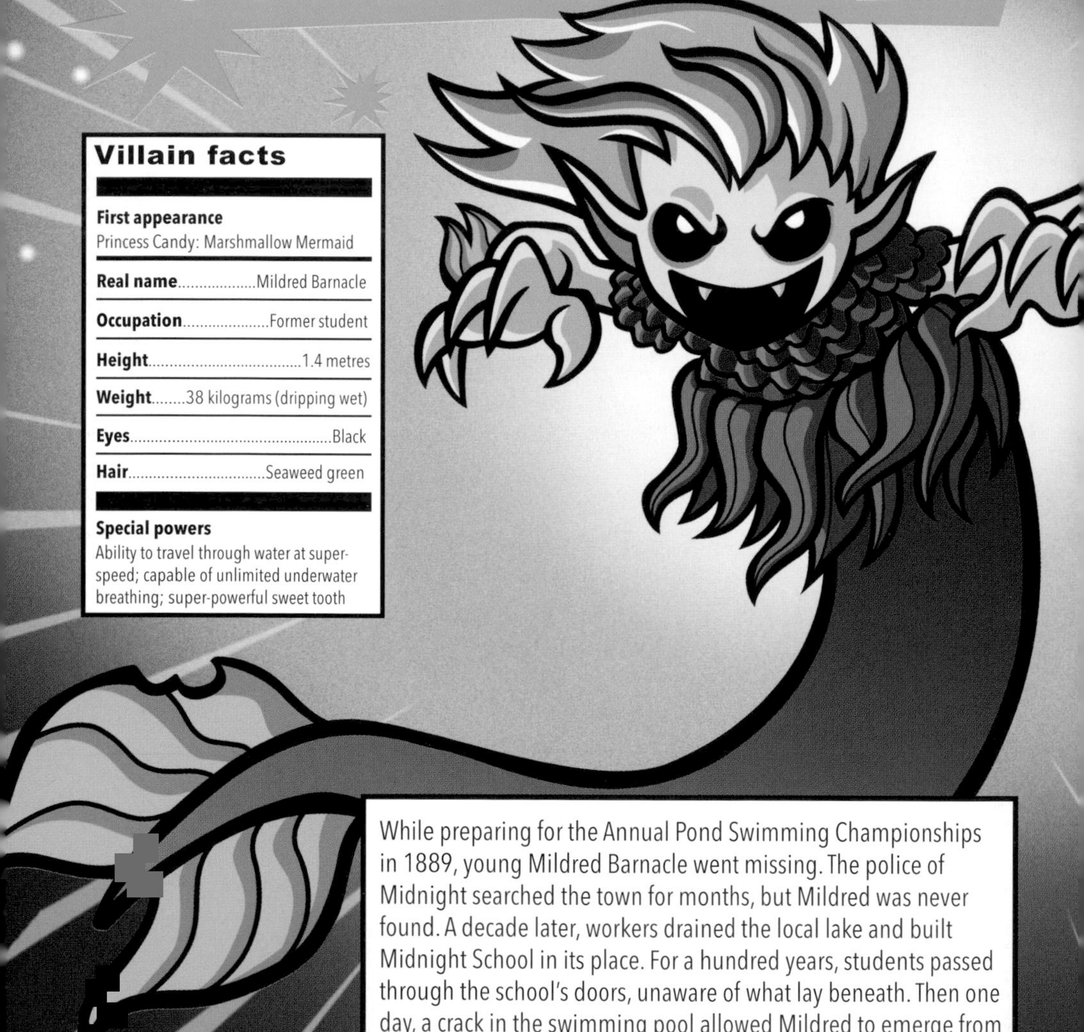

Villain facts

First appearance
Princess Candy: Marshmallow Mermaid

Real name..................Mildred Barnacle

Occupation....................Former student

Height....................................1.4 metres

Weight........38 kilograms (dripping wet)

Eyes...Black

Hair................................Seaweed green

Special powers
Ability to travel through water at super-speed; capable of unlimited underwater breathing; super-powerful sweet tooth

While preparing for the Annual Pond Swimming Championships in 1889, young Mildred Barnacle went missing. The police of Midnight searched the town for months, but Mildred was never found. A decade later, workers drained the local lake and built Midnight School in its place. For a hundred years, students passed through the school's doors, unaware of what lay beneath. Then one day, a crack in the swimming pool allowed Mildred to emerge from her watery grave. She had become the slippery and sweet-toothed . . . Marshmallow Mermaid!

AUNT PANDORA'S

PRINCESS PUZZLERS

Q: Who ate the first marshmallows?

A: Believe it or not, ancient Egyptian royalty snacked on marshmallows more than 4,000 years ago.

Q: Where did marshmallows get their funny name?

A: Egyptians made the first marshmallows from "mallow" plants, which are often found in swampy "marshes."

Q: Where is the marshmallow capital of the world?

A: In Ligonier, Indiana, USA, a marshmallow festival is held every year, with games and a marshmallow parade!

DISCUSSION QUESTIONS

1. Cody is allergic to marshmallows. Are you allergic to any types of food? If so, how do you deal with your allergy? If not, have you ever met anyone with a food allergy?

2. If Doozie Hiss was captured by the Marshmallow Mermaid, do you think Halo would save her? Why or why not?

3. At the end of the story, Halo escapes the Marshmallow Mermaid. Do you think the evil fish will ever return to Midnight School? Why or why not?

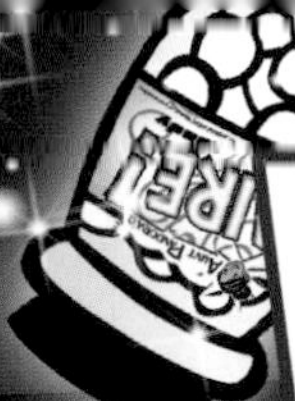

WRITING PROMPTS

1. Pretend your favourite sweets could turn you into a superhero. What would your superhero name be? What superpowers would you have? How would you use those powers?

2. Imagine you are the author. Write a second part to this story. Does the Marshmallow Mermaid come back? Does Cody win his swimming race?

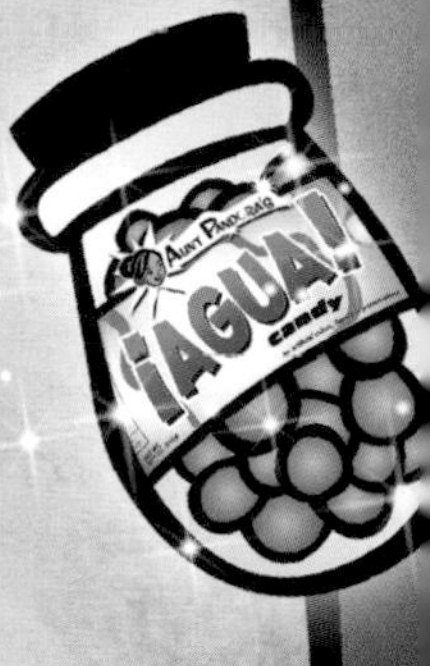
¡AGUA!
candy

3. Comics and graphic novels are often written and illustrated by two different people. Write a short story, and then give it to a friend to draw the pictures.

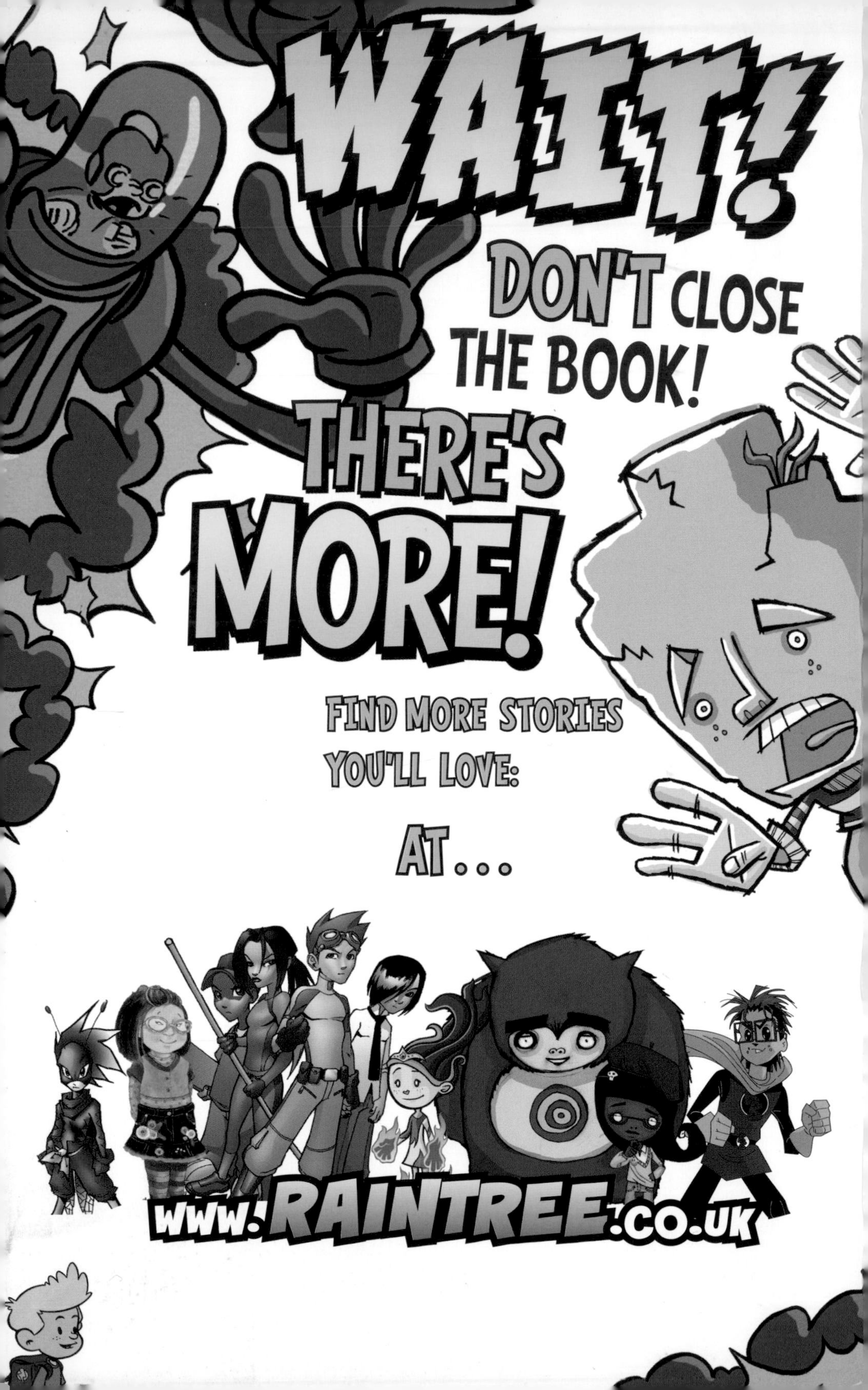
WAIT!
DON'T CLOSE THE BOOK!
THERE'S MORE!
FIND MORE STORIES YOU'LL LOVE:
AT...
WWW.RAINTREE.CO.UK